美国亚裔文学研究丛书

总主编　郭英剑

An Anthology of Japanese American Literature
美国日裔文学作品选

主编　郭英剑　王会刚　赵明珠

本研究受中国人民大学科学研究基金资助，系2017年度重大规划项目"美国亚裔文学研究"（编号：17XNLG10）阶段性成果。

中国人民大学出版社
·北京·

图书在版编目（CIP）数据

美国日裔文学作品选：英文 / 郭英剑，王会刚，赵明珠主编 .—北京：中国人民大学出版社，2022.10
（美国亚裔文学研究丛书 / 郭英剑总主编）
ISBN 978-7-300-31087-9

Ⅰ.①美… Ⅱ.①郭… ②王… ③赵… Ⅲ.①文学-作品综合集-美国-英文 Ⅳ.①I712.11

中国版本图书馆 CIP 数据核字（2022）第 184261 号

美国亚裔文学研究丛书
美国日裔文学作品选
总主编　郭英剑
主　编　郭英剑　王会刚　赵明珠
Meiguo Riyi Wenxue Zuopinxuan

出版发行	中国人民大学出版社			
社　址	北京中关村大街 31 号		邮政编码	100080
电　话	010-62511242（总编室）		010-62511770（质管部）	
	010-82501766（邮购部）		010-62514148（门市部）	
	010-62515195（发行公司）		010-62515275（盗版举报）	
网　址	http://www.crup.com.cn			
经　销	新华书店			
印　刷	唐山玺诚印务有限公司			
规　格	170 mm × 240 mm 16 开本		版　次	2022 年 10 月第 1 版
印　张	11.75		印　次	2022 年 10 月第 1 次印刷
字　数	216 000		定　价	68.00 元

版权所有　　侵权必究　　印装差错　　负责调换

总　序

美国亚裔文学的历史、现状与未来

郭英剑

一、何谓"美国亚裔文学"？

"美国亚裔文学"（Asian American Literature），简言之，是指由美国社会中的亚裔群体作家所创作的文学。也有人称之为"亚裔美国文学"。

然而，"美国亚裔文学"这个由两个核心词汇——"美国亚裔"和"文学"——所组成的术语，远没有它看上去那么简单。说它极其复杂，一点也不为过。因此，要想对"美国亚裔文学"有基本的了解，就需要从其中的两个关键词入手。

首先，"美国亚裔"中的"亚裔"，是指具有亚裔血统的美国人，但其所指并非一个单一的族裔，其组成包括美国来自亚洲各国（或者与亚洲各国有关联）的人员群体及其后裔，比如美国华裔（Chinese Americans）、日裔（Japanese Americans）、菲律宾裔（Filipino Americans）、韩裔（Korean Americans）、越南裔（Vietnamese Americans）、印度裔（Indian Americans）、泰国裔（Thai Americans）等等。

根据联合国的统计，亚洲总计有 48 个国家。因此，所谓"美国亚裔"自然包括在美国的所有这 48 个亚洲国家的后裔，或者有其血统的人员。由此所涉及的各国（以及地区）迥异的语言、不同的文化、独特的人生体验，以及群体交叉所产生的多样性，包括亚洲各国由于战争交恶所带给后裔及其有关人员的深刻影响，就构成了"美国亚裔"这一群体具有的极端复杂性。在美国统计局的定义中，美国亚裔是细分为"东亚"（East Asia）、"东南亚"（Southeast Asia）和南亚（South Asia）。[1] 当然，也正由于其复杂性，到现在有些亚洲国家在美国的后裔或者移民，尚未形成一个相对固定的族裔群体。

1　参见: Humes, Karen R, Jones, Nicholas A, Ramirez, Roberto R (March 2011). "Overview of Race and Hispanic Origin: 2010" (PDF). United States Census Bureau. U.S. Department of Commerce.

其次，文学主要由作家创作而成，由于"美国亚裔"群体的复杂性，自然导致"美国亚裔"的"作家"群体同样处于极其复杂的状态，但也因此使这一群体的概念具有相当大的包容性。凡是身在美国的亚裔后裔、具有亚洲血统或者后来移民美国的亚裔作家，都可以称之为"美国亚裔作家"。

由于亚裔群体的语言众多，加上一些移民作家的母语并非英语，因此，"美国亚裔文学"一般指的是美国亚裔作家使用英语所创作的文学作品。但由于历史的原因，学术界也把最早进入美国时，亚裔用本国语言所创作的文学作品，无论是口头作品还是文字作品——比如19世纪中期，华人进入美国时遭到拘禁时所创作的诗句，也都纳入"美国亚裔文学"的范畴之内。同时，随着全球化时代的到来，各国之间的文学与文化交流日益加强，加之移民日渐增加，因此，也将部分发表时为亚洲各国语言，但后来被翻译成英语的文学作品，同样纳入"美国亚裔文学"的范畴。

最后，"美国亚裔"的划分，除了语言、历史、文化之外，还有一个地理的因素需要考虑。随着时间的推移与学术界研究，特别是离散研究（Diaspora Studies）的进一步深化，"美国亚裔"中的"美国"（America），也不单单指"the United States"了。我们知道，由于全球化时代所带来的人口流动性的极度增加，国与国之间的界限有时候变得模糊起来，人们的身份也变得日益具有多样性和流动性。比如，由于经济全球化的原因，美国已不单单是一个地理概念上的美国。经济与文化的构成，造就了可口可乐、麦当劳等商业品牌，它们都已经变成了流动的美国的概念。这样的美国不断在"侵入"其他国家，并对其他国家产生了巨大的影响。当然，一个作家的流动性，也无形中扩大了"美国"的概念。比如，一个亚洲作家可能移民到美国，但一个美国亚裔作家也可能移民到其他国家。这样的流动性拓展了"美国亚裔"的定义与范畴。

为此，"美国亚裔文学"这一概念，有时候也包括一些身在美洲地区，但与美国有关联的作家，他们用英语进行创作；或者被翻译成英语的文学作品，也会被纳入这一范畴之内。

应该指出的是，由于"亚裔"群体进入美国的时间早晚不同，加上"亚裔"群体的复杂性，那么，每一个"亚裔"群体，都有其独有的美国族裔特征，比如华裔与日裔有所不同，印度裔与日裔也有所不同。如此一来，正如一些学者所认为那样，各个族裔的特征最好应该分开来叙述和加以研究。[2]

---

2 参见：Chin, Frank, et al. 1991. "Preface" to *Aiiieeeee! An Anthology of Asian American Writers*. Edited by Frank China, Jeffery Paul Chan, Lawson Fusao Inada, and Shawn Wong. A Mentor Book. p.xi.

二、为何要研究"美国亚裔文学"?

虽然上文中提出,"美国亚裔"是个复杂而多元的群体,"美国亚裔文学"包含了极具多样化的亚裔群体作家,但是我们还是要把"美国亚裔文学"当作一个整体来进行研究。理由有三:

首先,"美国亚裔文学"与"美国亚裔作家"(Asian American Writers)最早出现时,即是作为一个统一的概念而提出的。1974年,赵健秀(Frank Chin)等学者出版了《哎咿!美国亚裔作家选集》。[3] 作为首部划时代的"美国亚裔作家"的文学作品选集,该书通过发现和挖掘此前50年中被遗忘的华裔、日裔与菲律宾裔中的重要作家,选取其代表性作品,进而提出要建立作为独立的研究领域的"美国亚裔文学"(Asian American Literature)。[4]

其次,在亚裔崛起的过程中,无论是亚裔的无心之为,还是美国主流社会与其他族裔的有意为之,亚裔都是作为一个整体被安置在一起的。因此,亚裔文学也是作为一个整体而存在的。近年来,我国的"美国华裔文学"研究成为美国文学研究学界的一个热点。但在美国,虽然有"美国华裔文学"(Chinese American Literature)的说法,但真正作为学科存在的,则是"美国亚裔文学"(Asian American Literature),甚至更多的则是"美国亚裔研究"(Asian American Studies)。

再次,1970年代之后,"美国亚裔文学"的发展在美国学术界逐渐成为研究的热点,引发了研究者的广泛关注,为此,包括耶鲁大学、哥伦比亚大学、布朗大学、宾夕法尼亚大学等常青藤盟校以及斯坦福大学、加州大学系统的伯克利分校、洛杉矶分校等美国众多高校,都设置了"美国亚裔研究"(Asian American Studies)专业,也设置了"美国亚裔学系"(Department of Asian American Studies)或者"亚裔研究中心",开设了丰富多彩的亚裔文学与亚裔研究方面的课程。包括哈佛大学在内的众多高校也都陆续开设了众多的美国亚裔研究以及美国亚裔文学的课程,学术研究成果丰富多彩。

那么,我们需要提出的一个问题是,在中国语境下,研究"美国亚裔文学"的意义与价值究竟何在?我的看法如下:

第一,"美国亚裔文学"是"美国文学"的重要组成部分。不研究亚裔文学或者忽视甚至贬低亚裔文学,学术界对于美国文学的研究就是不完整的。如上文所说,亚裔文学的真正兴起是在20世纪六七十年代。美国六七十年代特殊的时

---

[3] Chin, Frank, Chan, Jeffery Paul, Inada, Lawson Fusao, et al. 1974. *Aiiieeeee! An Anthology of Asian-American Writers*. Howard University Press.

[4] 参见: Chin, Frank, et al. 1991. "Preface" to *Aiiieeeee! An Anthology of Asian American Writers*. Edited by Frank Chin, Jeffery Paul Chan, Lawson Fusao Inada, and Shawn Wong. A Mentor Book. pp.xi–xxii.

代背景极大促进了亚裔文学发展，自此，亚裔文学作品层出不穷，包括小说、戏剧、传记、短篇小说、诗歌等各种文学形式。在当下的美国，亚裔文学及其研究与亚裔的整体生存状态息息相关；种族、历史、人口以及政治诉求等因素促使被总称为"亚裔"的各个少数族裔联合发声，以期在美国政治领域和主流社会达到最大的影响力与辐射度。对此，学术界不能视而不见。

第二，我国现有的"美国华裔文学"研究，无法替代更不能取代"美国亚裔文学"研究。自从1980年代开始译介美国亚裔文学以来，我国国内的研究就主要集中在华裔文学领域，研究对象也仅为少数知名华裔作家及长篇小说创作领域。相较于当代国外亚裔文学研究的全面与广博，国内对于亚裔的其他族裔作家的作品关注太少。即使是那些亚裔文学的经典之作，如菲律宾裔作家卡罗斯·布鲁桑（Carlos Bulosan）的《美国在我心中》（*America Is in the Heart*, 1946），日裔女作家山本久惠（Hisaye Yamamoto）的《第十七个音节及其他故事》（*Seventeen Syllables and Other Stories*, 1949）、日裔约翰·冈田（John Okada）的《不－不仔》（*NO-NO Boy*, 1959），以及如今在美国文学界如日中天的青年印度裔作家裘帕·拉希莉（Jhumpa Lahiri）的作品，专题研究均十分少见。即便是像华裔作家任璧莲（Gish Jen）这样已经受到学者很大关注和研究的作家，其长篇小说之外体裁的作品同样没有得到足够的重视，更遑论国内学术界对亚裔文学在诗歌、戏剧方面的研究了。换句话说，我国学术界对于整个"美国亚裔文学"的研究来说还很匮乏，属于亟待开发的领域。实际上，在我看来，不研究"美国亚裔文学"，也无法真正理解"美国华裔文学"。

第三，在中国"一带一路"倡议与中国文化走出去的今天，作为美国文学研究的新型增长点，大力开展"美国亚裔文学"研究，特别是研究中国的亚洲周边国家如韩国、日本、印度等国在美国移民状况的文学表现，以及与华裔在美国的文学再现，使之与美国和世界其他国家的"美国亚裔文学"保持同步发展，具有较大的理论意义与学术价值。

三、"美国亚裔文学"及其研究：历史与现状

历史上看，来自亚洲国家的移民进入美国，可以追溯到18世纪。但真正开始较大规模的移民则是到了19世纪中后期。然而，亚裔从进入美国一开始，就遭遇到来自美国社会与官方的阻力与法律限制。从1880年代到1940年代这半个多世纪的岁月中，为了保护美国本土而出台的一系列移民法，都将亚洲各国人民排除在外，禁止他们当中的大部分人进入美国大陆地区。直到20世纪40至60年代移民法有所改革时，这种状况才有所改观。其中的改革措施之一就是取消了

国家配额。如此一来，亚洲移民人数才开始大规模上升。2010年的美国国家统计局分析显示，亚裔是美国社会移民人数增长最快的少数族裔。[5]

"美国亚裔"实际是个新兴词汇。这个词汇的创立与诞生实际上已经到了1960年代后期。在此之前，亚洲人或者具有亚洲血统者通常被称为"Oriental"（东方人）、"Asiatic"（亚洲人）和"Mongoloid"（蒙古人、黄种人）。[6] 美国历史学家市冈裕次（Yuji Ichioka）在1960年代末期，开创性地开始使用Asian American这个术语，[7] 从此，这一词汇开始被人普遍接受和广泛使用。

与此时间同步，"美国亚裔文学"在随后的1970年代作为一个文学类别开始出现并逐步产生影响。1974年，有两部著作几乎同时出版，都以美国亚裔命名。一部是《美国亚裔传统：散文与诗歌选集》，[8] 另外一部则是前面提到过的《哎咿！美国亚裔作家选集》。[9] 这两部著作，将过去长期被人遗忘的亚裔文学带到了聚光灯下，让人们仿佛看到了一种新的文学形式。其后，新的亚裔作家不断涌现，文学作品层出不穷。

最初亚裔文学的主要主题与主要内容为种族（race）、身份（identity）、亚洲文化传统、亚洲与美国或者西方国家之间的文化冲突，当然也少不了性别（sexuality）、社会性别（gender）、性别歧视、社会歧视等。后来，随着移民作家的大规模出现，离散文学的兴起，亚裔文学也开始关注移民、语言、家国、想象、全球化、劳工、战争、帝国主义、殖民主义等问题。

如果说，上述1974年的两部著作代表着亚裔文学进入美国文学的世界版图之中，那么，1982年著名美国亚裔研究专家金惠经（Elaine Kim）的《美国亚裔文学的创作及其社会语境》[10] 的出版，作为第一部学术著作，则代表着美国亚裔文学研究正式登上美国学术界的舞台。自此以后，不仅亚裔文学创作兴盛起来，而且亚裔文学研究也逐渐成为热点，成果不断推陈出新。

同时，人们对于如何界定"美国亚裔文学"等众多问题进行了深入的探讨，

---

5 参见：Wikipedia 依据"U.S. Census Show Asians Are Fastest Growing Racial Group"（NPR.org）所得出的数据统计。https://en.wikipedia.org/wiki/Asian_Americans。

6 Mio, Jeffrey Scott, ed. 1999. *Key Words in Multicultural Interventions: A Dictionary*. ABC-Clio ebook. Greenwood Publishing Group, p. 20.

7 K. Connie Kang, "Yuji Ichioka, 66; Led Way in Studying Lives of Asian Americans," *Los Angeles Times*, September 7, 2002. Reproduced at ucla.edu by the Asian American Studies Center.

8 Wand, David Hsin-fu, ed. 1974. *Asian American Heritage: An Anthology of Prose and Poetry*. New York: Pocket Books.

9 Chin, Frank, Chan, Jeffery Paul, I nada, Lawson Fusao, et al. 1974. *Aiiieeeee! An Anthology of Asian-American Writers*. Howard University Press.

10 Kim, Elaine. 1982. *Asian American Literature: An Introduction to the Writings and Their Social Context*. Philadelphia: Temple University Press.

进一步推动了这一学科向前发展。相关问题包括：究竟谁可以说自己是美国亚裔（an Asian America）？这里的America是不是就是单指"美国"（the United States）？是否可以包括"美洲"（Americas）？如果亚裔作家所写的内容与亚裔无关，能否算是"亚裔文学"？如果不是亚裔作家，但所写内容与亚裔有关，能否算在"亚裔文学"之内？

总体上看，早期的亚裔文学研究专注于美国身份的建构，即界定亚裔文学的范畴，以及争取其在美国文化与美国文学中应得的席位，是20世纪七八十年代亚裔民权运动的前沿阵地。早期学者如赵健秀、徐忠雄（Shawn Wong）等为领军人物。随后出现的金惠经、张敬珏（King-Kok Cheung）、骆里山（Lisa Lowe）等人均成为了亚裔文学研究领域的权威学者，他/她们的著作影响并造就了第二代美国亚裔文学研究者。20世纪90年代之后的亚裔文学研究逐渐淡化了早期研究中对于意识形态的侧重，开始向传统的学科分支、研究方法以及研究理论靠拢，研究视角多集中在学术马克思主义（academic Marxism）、后结构主义、后殖民、女权主义以及心理分析等。

进入21世纪以来，"美国亚裔文学"研究开始向多元化、全球化与跨学科方向发展。随着亚裔文学作品爆炸式的增长，来自阿富汗、印度、巴基斯坦、越南等族裔作家的作品开始受到关注，极大丰富与拓展了亚裔文学研究的领域。当代"美国亚裔文学"研究的视角与方法也不断创新，战争研究、帝国研究、跨国研究、视觉文化理论、空间理论、身体研究、环境理论等层出不穷。新的理论与常规性研究交叉进行，不但开创了新的研究领域，对于经典问题（例如身份建构）的研究也提供了新的解读方式与方法。

四、作为课题的"美国亚裔文学"研究及其丛书

"美国亚裔文学"研究，是由我担任课题负责人的2017年度中国人民大学科学研究基金重大规划项目。"美国亚裔文学研究丛书"，即是该项课题的结题成果。作为"美国亚裔文学"方面的系列丛书，将由文学史、文学作品选、文学评论集、学术论著等组成，由我担任该丛书的总主编。

"美国亚裔文学"研究在2017年4月立项。随后，该丛书的论证计划，得到了国内外专家的一致认可。2017年5月27日，中国人民大学科学研究基金重大规划项目"美国亚裔文学研究"开题报告会暨"美国亚裔文学研究高端论坛"在中国人民大学隆重召开。参加此次会议的专家学者全部为美国亚裔文学研究领域中的顶尖学者，包括美国加州大学洛杉矶分校的张敬珏教授、南京大学海外教育学院前院长程爱民教授、南京大学海外教育学院院长赵文书教授、北京语言大学

应用外语学院院长陆薇教授、北京外国语大学潘志明教授、解放军外国语学院石平萍教授等。在此次会议上，我向与会专家介绍了该项目的基本情况、未来研究方向与预计出版成果。与会专家对该项目的设立给予高度评价，强调在当今时代加强"美国亚裔文学"研究的必要性，针对该项目的预计研究及其成果，也提出了一些很好的建议。

根据最初的计划，这套丛书将包括文学史 2 部：《美国亚裔文学史》和《美国华裔文学史》；文学选集 2 部：《美国亚裔文学作品选》和《美国华裔文学作品选》；批评文选 2 部：《美国亚裔文学评论集》和《美国华裔文学评论集》；访谈录 1 部：《美国亚裔作家访谈录》；学术论著 3 部，包括美国学者张敬珏教授的《静默留声》和《文心无界》。总计 10 部著作。

根据我的基本设想，《美国亚裔文学史》和《美国华裔文学史》的撰写，将力图体现研究者对美国亚裔文学的研究进入到了较为深入的阶段。由于文学史是建立在研究者对该研究领域发展变化的总体认识上，涉及文学流派、创作方式、文学与社会变化的关系、作家间的关联等各方面的问题，我们试图通过对亚裔文学发展进行总结和评价，旨在为当前亚裔文学和华裔文学的研究和推广做出一定贡献。

《美国亚裔文学作品选》和《美国华裔文学作品选》，除了记录、介绍等基本功能，还将在一定程度上发挥形成民族认同、促进意识形态整合等功能。作品选编是民族共同体想象性构建的重要途径，也是作为文学经典得以确立和修正的最基本方式之一。因此，这样的作品选编，也要对美国亚裔文学的研究起到重要的促进作用。

《美国亚裔文学评论集》和《美国华裔文学评论集》，将主要选编美国、中国以及世界上最有学术价值的学术论文，虽然有些可能因为版权问题而不得不舍弃，但我们努力使之成为中国学术界研究"美国亚裔文学"和"美国华裔文学"的重要参考书目。

《美国亚裔作家访谈录》、美国学者的著作汉译、中国学者的美国亚裔文学学术专著等，将力图促使中美两国学者之间的学术对话，特别是希望中国的"美国亚裔文学"研究，既在中国的美国文学研究界，也要在美国和世界上的美国文学研究界发出中国学者的声音。"一带一路"倡议的实施，使得文学研究的关注发生了转变，从过分关注西方话语，到逐步转向关注中国（亚洲）话语，我们的美国亚裔（华裔）文学研究，正是从全球化视角切入，思考美国亚裔（华裔）文学的世界性。

2018 年，我们按照原计划出版了《美国亚裔文学作品选》《美国华裔文学作品选》《美国亚裔文学评论集》《美国华裔文学评论集》。2022年上半年，我们出版了学术专著《文心无界——不拘性别、文类与形式的华美文学》。2022年下半年，还将出版《美国日裔文学作品选》《美国韩裔文学作品选》《美国越南裔文学作品选》《美国西亚裔文学作品选》《美国南亚裔文学作品选》等5部文学选集。

需要说明的是，这5部选集是在原有计划之外的产物。之所以在《美国亚裔文学作品选》之外又专门将其中最主要的国家与区域的文学作品结集出版，是因为在研究过程中我发现，现有的《美国亚裔文学作品选》已经无法涵盖丰富多彩的亚裔文学。更重要的是，无论是在国内还是在美国，像这样将美国亚裔按照国别与区域划分后的文学作品选全部是空白，国内外学术界对这些国别与区域的文学创作的整体关注也较少，可以说它们都属于亟待开垦的新研究领域。通过这5部选集，可以让国内对于美国亚裔文学有更为完整的了解。我也希望借此填补国内外在这个领域的空白。

等到丛书全部完成出版，将会成为一套由15部著作所组成的系列丛书。2018年的时候，我曾经把这套丛书界定为"国内第一套较为完整的美国亚裔文学方面的系列丛书"。现在，时隔4年之后，特别是在有了这新出版的5部选集之后，我可以说这套丛书将是"国内外第一套最为完整的美国亚裔文学方面的系列丛书"。

那么，我们为什么要对"美国亚裔文学"进行深入研究，并要编辑、撰写和翻译这套丛书呢？

首先，虽然"美国亚裔文学"在国外已有较大的影响，学术界也对此具有相当规模的研究，但在国内学术界，出于对"美国华裔文学"的偏爱与关注，"美国亚裔文学"相对还是一个较为陌生的领域。因此，本课题首次以"亚裔"集体的形式标示亚裔文学的存在，旨在介绍"美国亚裔文学"，推介具有族裔特色和代表性的作家作品。

其次，选择"美国亚裔文学"为研究对象，其中也有对"美国华裔文学"的研究，希望能够体现我们对全球化视野中华裔文学的关注，也体现试图融合亚裔、深入亚裔文学研究的学术自觉。同时，在多元化多种族的美国社会语境中，我们力主打破国内长久以来专注"美国华裔文学"研究的固有模式，转而关注包括华裔作家在内的亚裔作家所具有的世界性眼光。

最后，顺应美国亚裔文学发展的趋势，对美国亚裔文学的研究不仅是文学研究界的关注热点，还是我国外语与文学教育的关注焦点。我们希望为高校未来"美国亚裔文学"的课程教学，提供一套高水平的参考丛书。

五、"美国亚裔文学"及其研究的未来

如前所述,"美国亚裔文学"在20世纪70年代逐渐崛起后,使得亚裔文学从沉默走向了发声。到21世纪,亚裔文学呈现出多元化的发展特征,更重要的是,许多新生代作家开始崭露头角。单就这些新的亚裔作家群体,就有许多值得我们关注的话题。

2018年6月23日,"2018美国亚裔文学高端论坛——跨界:21世纪的美国亚裔文学"在中国人民大学隆重召开。参加会议的专家学者将近150人。

在此次会议上,我提出来:今天,为什么要研究美国亚裔文学?我们要研究什么?

正如我们在会议通知上所说,美国亚裔文学在一百多年的风雨沧桑中历经"沉默""觉醒",走向"发声",见证了美国亚裔族群的沉浮兴衰。21世纪以来,美国亚裔文学在全球冷战思维升温和战火硝烟不断的时空背景下,不囿于狭隘的种族主义藩篱,以"众声合奏"与"兼容并蓄"之势构筑出一道跨洋、跨国、跨种族、跨语言、跨文化、跨媒介、跨学科的文学景观,呈现出鲜明的世界主义意识。为此,我们拟定了一些主要议题。包括:1. 美国亚裔文学中的跨洋书写;2. 美国亚裔文学中的跨国书写;3. 美国亚裔文学中的跨种族书写;4. 美国亚裔文学中的跨语言书写;5. 美国亚裔文学中的跨文化书写;6. 美国亚裔文学的翻译跨界研究;7. 美国亚裔文学的跨媒介研究;8. 美国亚裔文学的跨学科研究等。

2019年6月22日,"2019美国亚裔文学高端论坛"在中国人民大学举行,会议的主题是"战争与和平:美国亚裔文学研究中的生命书写"。那次会议,依旧有来自中国的近80所高校的150余位教师和硕博研究生参加我们的论坛。

2020年年初,全球疫情大暴发,我们的"2020美国亚裔文学高端论坛"一直往后推迟,直到2020年12月5日在延边大学举行,会议的主题是"疫情之思:变局中的美国亚裔文学"。因为疫情原因,我们劝阻了很多愿意来参会的学者,但即便如此,也有近百位来自各地的专家学者与研究生前来参会。

2021年6月26—27日,"相遇与融合:2021首届华文/华裔文学研讨会"在西北师范大学举行。这次会议是由我在延边大学的会议上提出倡议,得到了中国社会科学院文学所赵稀方教授的积极响应,由他和我一起联合发起并主办,由西北师范大学外国语学院承办。我们知道,长期以来,华裔文学和华文文学分属不同的学科和研究领域,其研究对象、传统和范式都有所不同,但血脉相承的天然联系终究会让两者相遇、走向融合。从时下的研究看,虽然两者的研究范式自成体系、独树一帜,但都面临着华裔作家用中文创作和华人作家用外文创作的新趋势,这给双方的学科发展与研究领域都带来了新的挑战,也带来了新的学科发

展机遇。我们都相信，在学科交叉融合已成为实现创新发展必然趋势的当下语境中，华裔/华文文学走到了相遇与融合的最佳时机。为此，我们倡议并搭建平台，希望两个领域的学者同台进行学术交流与对话，探讨文学研究的新发展，以求实现华裔文学和华文文学的跨界融通。

事实上，21世纪以来，亚裔群体、亚裔所面临的问题、亚裔研究都发生了巨大的变化。从过去较为单纯的亚裔走向了跨越太平洋（transpacific）；从过去的彰显美国身份（claiming America）到今天的批评美国身份（critiquing America）；过去单一的America，现在变成了复数的Americas，这些变化都值得引起我们的高度重视。由此所引发的诸多问题，也需要我们去认真对待。比如：如何在"21世纪"这个特殊的时间区间内去理解"美国亚裔文学"这一概念？有关"美国亚裔文学"的概念构建，是否本身就存在着作家的身份焦虑与书写的界限划分？如何把握"美国亚裔文学"的整体性与区域性？"亚裔"身份是否是作家在表达过程中去主动拥抱的归属之地？等等。

2021年年底，国家社会科学基金重大招标课题揭晓，我申请的"美国族裔文学中的文化共同体思想研究"喜获中标。这将进一步推动我目前所从事的美国亚裔文学研究，并在未来由现在的美国亚裔文学研究走向美国的整个族裔文学研究。

展望未来，"美国亚裔文学"呈现出更加生机勃勃的生命力，"美国亚裔文学"的研究也将迎来更加光明的前途。

2018年8月28日定稿于哈佛大学
2022年8月28日修改于北京

前　言

"美国亚裔文学"研究，是由中国人民大学"杰出学者"特聘教授郭英剑先生担任课题负责人的2017年度中国人民大学科学研究基金重大规划项目。"美国亚裔文学研究丛书"，是该项课题的结题成果。由郭英剑教授担任该套丛书的总主编。这是国内第一套最为完整的"美国亚裔文学"方面的系列丛书，由文学史、文学作品选、文学评论集、学术论著等所组成。

所谓"美国日裔文学"，是指具有日本血统的美国人（即日裔）用英语创作的作品。此处的日裔，不仅包括在美国出生并在美国接受教育以及在美国出生回到日本接受教育后重返美国的本土日裔，还包括在美国领土之外出生后到达美国的移民作家（成年之后的移民者也包括在内），如卡尔·哈特曼、杉本钺子以及野口米次郎等一世作家。"美国日裔文学"的题材多是反映日裔在美国的生活经历，尤其是他们在第二次世界大战期间的拘留营经历。

"美国日裔文学"无疑是"美国亚裔文学"版图中不可或缺的一部分，它在一百多年的发展历程中不断壮大，成为美国少数族裔文学中的佼佼者。现在，美国日裔文学已然成为学者们了解美国社会历史，尤其是第二次世界大战期间美国社会状况的一个重要媒介。众多日裔作家在自己作品中揭露、控诉美国政府在第二次世界大战期间肆意践踏日裔公民的权利，这也促使美国社会开始反省自身。

日本人移民美国始于"明治维新"（1868年）之后，改革后的日本政府开始加强同西方发达国家的交往。为了维护自身形象，日本政府严格挑选赴美人员，并对他们进行一定的语言及文化培训，因此相较于华人而言，这些日本移民能够更好地适应并融入美国社会。这些一世（Issei，一般指1924年之前移民到美洲的日本人）很多都能熟练运用英语进行创作，同时日裔社区的各种报纸和杂志也为他们的创作提供了舞台。现在我们能够看到的早期用英语创作的日裔作家包括卡尔·哈特曼、杉本钺子以及野口米次郎等。其中最有影响力的当属卡尔·哈特曼，他赢得了美国主流文学界和艺术界的认同，不仅创作了大量的英语诗歌，还将"俳句"（Haiku）这一日本诗歌形式引介给美国读者。

第二次世界大战结束后，随着以森敏雄、山本久枝、约翰·冈田等人为代表的大批二世（Nisei）作家步入文坛，美国日裔文学迎来了大发展，进入了繁荣期。二世日裔作家群体数量大，文学成就也很高。二世作家的作品要么讲述一世父母以及二世子女的农场生活，反映他们之间的代际矛盾，要么叙述他们在第二次世界大战期间被拘禁关押的经历，控诉美国政府的野蛮行径。随着20世纪70年代美国多元文化的兴起，以劳森·稻田等人为代表的三世（Sansei）作家也开始崭露头角，登上历史舞台，使得美国日裔作家的队伍更加壮大。

《美国日裔文学作品选》以历史为发展脉络，精选了35位美国日裔作家的作品，并以作家的出生年代为顺序进行编目排列。"美国日裔文学"从属于"美国亚裔文学"，鉴于日益壮大的日裔作家及其出色的文学作品，我们认为需要将"日裔文学"单独列出，编写这部《美国日裔文学作品选》，便于人们了解更多日裔作家的创作。

本作品选试图最大程度反映美国日裔文学一个多世纪以来的发展历程与变化，力求能够反映抗争、代际冲突以及身份认同等美国日裔文学的重大议题。作品选中涉及的作家新老并存，彰显出美国日裔文学的发展步入繁荣阶段，同时也说明日裔文学发展后继有人。为了能更好地体现美国日裔文学发展的新动向，我们在作品选中也扩展了所选作品的体裁范围。作品选尽管仍然以小说、诗歌、戏剧等传统体裁为主，但在小说方面，我们也增加了儿童文学、科幻小说等门类。

遗憾的是，由于篇幅所限，《美国日裔文学作品选》中的部分作品只是节选片段，而且因为各种历史与现实的原因，一些作家的作品仍未能囊括其中，但通过这些选文展现出的冰山一角，大家可以继续探寻日裔文学的广袤空间。

无论如何，我们都希望《美国日裔文学作品选》能够成为中国学术界研究"美国亚裔文学"，特别是"美国日裔文学"的重要参考书目。

编　者

2022年8月28日

目　录

1. 卡尔·哈特曼（Carl Sadakichi Hartmann, 1867—1944）···································· 1
   - Nocturne ·· 2
   - Drifting Flowers of the Sea ·· 3
2. 杉本钺子（Etsu Inagaki Sugimoto, 1874—1950）······································ 5
   - *A Daughter of the Samurai* ·· 6
3. 野口米次郎（Yone Noguchi, 1875—1947）··· 10
   - *The American Diary of a Japanese Girl* ·· 11
4. 宫本和男（Kazuo Miyamoto, 1897—1988）··· 17
   - *Hawaii: End of the Rainbow* ·· 18
5. 森敏雄（Toshio Mori, 1910—1980）·· 22
   - *Yokohama, California* ·· 23
6. 梅内·大久保（Miné Okubo, 1912—2001）··· 27
   - *Citizen 13660* ·· 28
7. 莫妮卡·曾根（Monica Sone, 1919—2011）·· 34
   - *Nisei Daughter* ·· 35
8. 山本久枝（Hisaye Yamamoto, 1921—2011）·· 39
   - *The Brown House* ·· 40
9. 内田良子（Yoshiko Uchida, 1921—1992）·· 45
   - *Picture Bride* ··· 46
10. 约翰·冈田（John Okada, 1923—1971）··· 50
    - *No-No Boy* ·· 51

11. 弥尔顿·村山（Milton Murayama, 1923—2016） ········· 54
　　All I Asking for Is My Body ········· 55

12. 山内若子（Wakako Yamauchi, 1924—2018） ········· 58
　　The Music Lessons ········· 59

13. 珍妮·若月·休斯敦（Jeanne Wakatsuki Houston, 1934— ） ········· 62
　　Farewell to Manzanar ········· 63

14. 劳森·稻田（Lawson Fusao Inada, 1938— ） ········· 67
　　Legends from Camp ········· 68

15. 罗尼·金子（Lonny Kaneko, 1939—2017） ········· 71
　　The Shoyu Kid ········· 72

16. 伊川桃子（Momoko Iko, 1940— ） ········· 77
　　Gold Watch ········· 78

17. 美里木古（Janice Mirikitani, 1941—2021） ········· 82
　　Awake in the River ········· 83

18. 弗罗伦斯·爱·小川（Florence Ai Ogawa, 1947—2010） ········· 86
　　Killing Floor ········· 87

19. 山下凯伦（Karen Tei Yamashita, 1951— ） ········· 90
　　Brazil-Maru ········· 91

20. 菲利普·菅·五反田（Philip Kan Gotanda, 1951— ） ········· 97
　　Yankee Dawg You Die ········· 98

21. 加利特·本乡（Garrett Hongo, 1951— ） ········· 103
　　Volcano: A Memoir of Hawai'i ········· 104

22. 西尔维娅·渡边（Sylvia Watanabe, 1953— ） ········· 107
　　Talking to the Dead: Stories ········· 108

23. 大卫·村（David Mura, 1952— ） ········· 112
　　The Colors of Desire ········· 113

24. 辛西娅·角畑（Cynthia Kadohata, 1956— ） ········· 119
　　A Place to Belong ········· 120

25. 露丝·尾关（Ruth L. Ozeki, 1956— ） ········· 123
　　All over Creation ········· 124

26. 韦丽娜·芳须·休斯敦（Velina Hasu Houston, 1957— ）·················· 128
    Morning Has Broken ·· 129

27. 森京子（Kyoko Mori, 1957— ）·· 132
    Shizuko's Daughter ··· 133

28. 朱莉·大塚（Julie Otsuka, 1962— ）······································· 136
    When the Emperor Was Divine ··· 137

29. 妮娜·雷伏娃（Nina Revoyr, 1969— ）···································· 140
    Wingshooters ··· 141

30. 布伦达·肖内西（Brenda Shaughnessy, 1970— ）························ 143
    Our Andromeda ·· 144

31. 柳原垣谷（Hanya Yanagihara, 1975— ）·································· 146
    A Little Life ··· 147

32. 谷口裕子（Yuko Taniguchi, 1975— ）····································· 151
    Foreign Wife Elegy ·· 152

33. 凯蒂·北村（Katie Kitamura, 1979— ）···································· 153
    Intimacies ··· 154

34. 菲尔·凯伊（Phil Kaye, 1987— ）··· 158
    Date & Time ·· 159

35. 莎拉·凯（Sarah Kay, 1988— ）··· 163
    No Matter the Wreckage ·· 164

1

(Carl Sadakichi Hartmann, 1867—1944)
卡尔·哈特曼

作者简介

卡尔·哈特曼（Carl Sadakichi Hartmann，1867—1944）是美国日裔著名的诗人、艺术和摄影评论家。他出生于日本的长崎（Nagasaki），母亲是日本人，父亲是德国人。出生之后不久，哈特曼被带到德国汉堡，15岁之后定居在美国费城，并于1894年加入美国国籍。哈特曼是现代主义艺术的重要参与者，与著名诗人惠特曼、马拉美以及庞德有着密切的交往，被誉为"波西米亚之王"。他的诗歌作品包括《海上漂浮的花朵及其他作品》（*Drifting Flowers of the Sea and Other Poems*, 1904）以及《日本韵律》（*Japanese Rhythms*, 1915），这些诗歌作品均受到象征主义和东方文学的影响。与此同时，他还将"俳句"（Haiku）这一日本诗歌形式引介给美国读者，用英语创作了一系列俳句。哈特曼对各种艺术形式都很感兴趣，但是他似乎更加钟爱戏剧。哈特曼对各种艺术形式都很感兴趣，但是他似乎更加钟爱戏剧，创作了一系列的戏剧作品包括《孔子》（*Confucius: A Drama in Two Acts*, 1923）以及《纽约公寓里的悲剧》（*A Tragedy in a New York Flat: A Dramatic Episode in Two Scenes*, 1896）等。哈特曼的戏剧在主题和范围上都具有跨文化和国际化的特点，而这一特点在此后的美国亚裔戏剧中一直得到延续和发展。哈特曼的戏剧在主题和范围上都具有跨文化和国际化的特点，而这一特点在此后的美国亚裔戏剧中一直得到延续和发展。

下文所选的诗歌出自哈特曼的诗集《海上漂浮的花朵及其他作品》。《夜曲》一诗中，作者描写了夏夜的海洋、星星、沙滩以及梦想与希望。《海上漂浮的花朵》一诗则是描绘海上明月、波涛、花朵与希望。

作品选读

Nocturne

Upon the silent sea-swept land
    The dreams of night fall soft and gray,
        The waves fade on the jeweled sand
            Like some lost hope of yesterday.

The dreams of night fall soft and gray
Upon the summer-colored seas,
    Like some lost hope of yesterday,
        The sea-mow's song is on the breeze.

Upon the summer-colored seas
        Sails gleam and glimmer ghostly white,
           The sea-mow's song is on the breeze
                Lost in the monotone of night.

Sails gleam and glimmer ghostly white,
    They come and slowly drift away,
        Lost in the monotone of night,
            Like visions of a summer-day.

They shift and slowly drift away
    Like lovers' lays that wax and wane,
The visions of a summer-day
    Whose dreams we ne'er will dream again.

Like lovers' lays that wax and wane
    The star dawn shifts from sail to sail,
    Like dreams we ne'er will dream again;
        The sea-mews follow on their trail.

The star dawn shifts from sail to sail,
As they drift to the dim unknow,
   The sea-mews follow on their trail
   In quest of some dreamland zone.

In quest of some far dreamland zone,
   Of some far silent sea-swept land,
     They are lost in the dim unknow,
     Where waves fade on jeweled sand
        And dreams of night fall soft and gray,
     Like some lost hope of yesterday.

Drifting Flowers of the Sea

Across the dunes, in the waning light,
The rising moon pours her amber rays,
Through the slumberous air of the dim, brown night
The pungent smell of the seaweed strays—
   From vast and trackless spaces
     Where wind and water meet,
       White flowers, that rise from the sleepless deep,
         Come drifting to my feet.
       They flutter the shore in a drowsy tune,
         Unfurl their bloom to the lightlorn sky,
           Allow a caress to the rising moon,
              Then fall to slumber, and fade, and die.

White flowers, a-bloom on the vagrant deep,
Like dreams of love, rising out of sleep,
You are the songs, I dreamt out never sung,
Pale hopes my thoughts alone have known,
Vain words ne'er uttered, though on the tongue,
That winds to the sibilant seas have blown.
   In you, I see the everlasting drift of years
     That will endure all sorrows, smiles and tears;

> For when the bell of time will ring the doom
> To all the follies of human race,
> You still will rise in fugitive bloom
> And garland the shores of ruined space.

2

(Etsu Inagaki Sugimoto, 1874—1950)
杉本钺子

作者简介

  杉本钺子（Etsu Inagaki Sugimoto, 1874—1950）出生于日本长冈市一个没落武士家庭，是著名美国日裔自传作家和小说家。她在东京的基督教学校完成教育后，以包办婚姻的形式嫁给美国辛辛那提的一个日本商人从而移民到美国。丈夫去世之后，她带着两个女儿回到日本，后来又回到美国以便女儿接受美式教育。杉本长期居住在纽约，她在哥伦比亚大学教授日本语言、文化以及历史，也为一些报纸、杂志撰写文章。她最著名的作品是《武士的女儿》(*A Daughter of the Samurai*, 1925)。在这部自传中，杉本钺子讲述了自己在日美两种文化中的成长经历。杉本的作品"具有很强的浪漫主义怀旧色彩和日本民族特征"，她将自己视为日本和美国之间的"文化大使"，通过自己的作品向美国读者介绍日本文化。而从杉本的小说来看，她似乎安于拥有一个可以向自己的美国同胞解说日本生活方式的日本身份。

  在《武士的女儿》的第一部分中，杉本回顾了自己在日本的童年时代，她所接受的教育、日本的社会和文化习俗以及她被灌输的忠诚、勇敢和荣誉等价值观，这些价值观是武士精神的特征。自传的第二部分讲述了杉本和她的日本商人丈夫在加利福尼亚的生活，以及她在丈夫死后被迫回到日本的故事。故事以她和女儿们永久地回到美国为终结。

  节选部分为自传的第一章，作者主要回忆了自己的故乡长冈。

作品选读

A Daughter of the Samurai

I Winters in Echigo
(Excerpt)

Japan is often called by foreign people a land of sunshine and cherry blossoms. This is because tourists generally visit only the eastern and southern parts of the country, where the climate is mild all the year round. On the northwest coast the winters are long, snow often covering the ground from December to March or April.

In the province of Echigo, where was my home, winter usually began with a heavy snow which came down fast and steady until only the thick, round ridgepoles of our thatched roofs could be seen. Then groups of coolies, with straw mats over their shoulders and big woven hats that looked like umbrellas, came and with broad wooden shovels cut tunnels through from one side of the street to the other. The snow was not removed from the middle of the street all winter. It lay in a long pile, towering far above the housetops. The coolies cut steps, for they were carrying snow at intervals all winter, and we children used to climb up and run along the top. We played many games there, sometimes pretending we were knights rescuing a snowbound village, or fierce brigands stealing upon it for an attack.

But a still more exciting time for us was before the snow came, when the entire town was making preparations for winter. This always took several weeks, and each day as we went to and from school we would stop to watch the coolies busily wrapping the statues and small shrines along the streets in their winter clothing of straw. The stone lanterns and all the trees and bushes of our gardens were enclosed in straw, and even the outside walls of the temples were protected by sheets of matting fastened on with strips of bamboo, or immense nettings made of straw rope. Every day the streets presented a new appearance, and by the time the big carved lions at the temple steps were covered, we were a city of grotesque straw tents of every shape and size, waiting for the snow that would bury us in for three or four months.

Most large houses had thatched roofs with wide eaves, but the shops on the streets had shingled roofs weighted with stones to prevent avalanches when the snow began to melt in the spring. Above all the sidewalks extended a permanent roof, and during the winter the sidewalks were enclosed by walls of upright boards with an occasional panel of oiled paper, which turned them into long halls, where we could walk all over town in the stormiest weather, entirely protected from wind and snow. These halls were dim, but not dark, for light shines through snow pretty well, and even at the street corners, where we crossed through the snow tunnels, it was light enough for us to read good-sized characters. Many a time, coming home from school, I have read my lessons in the tunnel, pretending that I was one of the ancient sages who studied by snow-light.

Echigo, which means "Behind the Mountains," is so shut off from the rest of Japan by the long Kiso range that during the early feudal days it was considered by the Government only a frozen outpost suitable as a place of exile for offenders too strong in position or influence to be treated as criminals. To this class belonged to reformers. In those days Japan had little tolerance for reforms either in politics or religion, and an especially progressive thinker at court or a broad-minded monk was branded as equally obnoxious and sent to some desolate spot where his ambitions would be permanently crushed. Most political offenders that were sent to Echigo either filled the graves of the little cemetery beyond the execution ground or lost themselves in some simple home among the peasants. Our literature holds many a pathetic tale of some rich and titled youth, who, disguised as a pilgrim, wanders through the villages of Echigo, searching for his lost father.

The religious reformers fared better; for they generally spent their lives in working quietly and inoffensively among the people. Some founders of new Buddhist sects exiled for a lifetime, were men of great ability, and gradually their belief spread so widely that Echigo became known all over Japan as the stronghold of reformed Buddhism. From earliest childhood I was familiar with priest tales and was accustomed to seeing pictures of images cut on the rocks or carved figures standing in caves on the mountainsides—the work of the tireless hands of those ancient monks.

My home was in the old castle town of Nagaoka. Our household consisted of my father and mother, my honored grandmother, my brother, my sister, and myself. Then there was Jiya, my father's head servant, and my nurse, Ishi, besides Kin and Toshi. Several other old servants came and went on occasions. I had married sisters, all in distant homes except the eldest, who lived about half a day's jinrikisha ride from Nagaoka. She came occasionally to visit us, and sometimes I went home with her to spend several days in her big thatched farmhouse, which had been, in ancient days, the fortress of three mountains. Samurai families often married into the farmer class, which was next in rank to the military, and much respected, for "one who owns rice villages holds the life of the nation in his hand."

We lived just on the edge of the town in a huge, rambling house that had been added to from time to time ever since I could remember. As a result, the heavy thatched roof sagged at the gable joinings, the plaster walls had numerous jogs and patches, and the many rooms of various sizes were connected by narrow, crooked halls that twisted about in a most unexpected manner. Surrounding the house, but some distance away, was a high wall of broken boulders, topped with a low, solid fence of wood. The roof of the gateway had tipped-up corners, and patches of moss on the brown thatch. It was supported by immense posts between which swung wooden gates with ornamental iron hinges that reached halfway across the heavy boards. On each side there extended, for a short distance, a plaster wall pierced by a long, narrow window with wooden bars. The gates were always open during the day, but if at night there came knocking and the call "Tano-mo-o! Tano-mo-o!" (I ask to enter!) even in the well-known voice of a neighbour, Jiya was so loyal to old-time habit that he invariably ran to peep through one of these windows before opening the gate to the guest.

From the gateway to the house was a walk of large, uneven stones, in the wide cracks of which grew the first foreign flowers that I ever saw—short-stemmed, round-headed little things that Jiya called "giant's buttons." Someone had given him the seed; and as he considered no foreign flower worthy of the dignity of a place in our garden, he cunningly planted them where they would be trod upon by our disrespectful feet. But they were hardy plants and grew as luxuriantly as moss.

That our home was such a makeshift was the result of one of the tragedies of the Restoration. Echigo Province was one of those that had believed in the dual government. To our people, the Mikado was too sacred to be in touch with war, or even annoying civil matters, and so they fought to uphold the shogun power to which, for generations, their ancestors had been loyal. At which time my father was a karo, or first counsellor of the daimiate of Nagaoka, a position which he had held since the age of seven, when the sudden death of my grandfather had left it vacant. Because of certain unusual circumstances, my father was the only executive in power, and thus it was that during the wars of the Restoration he had the responsibility and the duties of the office of daimio.

At the bitterest moment that Nagaoka ever knew, Echigo found herself on the defeated side. When my mother learned that her husband's cause was lost and he taken prisoner, she sent her household to a place of safety, and then, to prevent the mansion from falling into the hands of the enemy, she with her own hands set fire to it and from the mountainside watched it burn to the ground.

After the stormy days of war were past and Father finally was free from the governorship which he had been directed to retain until the central government became stabilized, he gathered together the remains of his family estate, and after sharing with his now "fish-on-land" retainers, he built this temporary home on the site of his former mansion. Then he planted a mulberry grove on a few acres of land nearby and prided himself on having levelled his rank to the class of farmer. Men of samurai rank knew nothing about business. It had always been considered a disgrace for them to handle money; so the management of all business affairs was left to faithful but wholly inexperienced Jiya, while Father devoted his life to reading, to memories, and to introducing unwelcome ideas of progressive reform to his less advanced neighbours.

3

(Yone Noguchi, 1875—1947)
野口米次郎

作者简介

野口米次郎（Yone Noguchi，1875—1947）是著名美国日裔诗人、小说家以及文学评论家。他出生于日本名古屋（Nagoya）的对马市（Tsushima），就读于东京的庆应义塾大学（Keio University）。1893年，野口离开日本前往美国旧金山。在旧金山期间，野口曾在加州帕洛阿尔托（Palo Alto）的一所斯坦福大学（Stanford University）预科学校学习了几个月，也从事过新闻工作，加入了一批日本流亡者经营的报纸。野口励志成为一名诗人，与旧金山湾区的诗人杰昆·米勒（Joaquin Miller）、格列特·伯吉斯（Gelett Burgess）等人交往甚密。在1900年前往美国东部地区之前，他一直是湾区文学界的重要人物。1900年后，野口先后到达芝加哥、纽约、华盛顿特区等地，其间也曾经到英国旅行，结识了威廉·巴特勒·叶芝（William Butler Yeats）、托马斯·哈代（Thomas Hardy）等英国著名文学家。1904年，野口回到日本，并担任母校庆应义塾大学英文系教授。在日本期间，他发表了大量的文学评论文章，并用英文出版大量著作，向西方人介绍日本文化，同时向日本人介绍西方文化。1913年他再次前往英国，并在牛津大学的莫德林学院（Magdalen College）讲授日本文学。1919—1920年间，他又前往美国，在斯坦福大学、加州大学伯克利分校、芝加哥大学和犹他大学以及多伦多大学等地发表演讲。1947年，野口米次郎在日本去世。

野口的作品很多，主要包括小说《日本女孩的美国日记》（*The American Diary of a Japanese Girl*, 1902）及其续集《日本侍女的美国信件》（*The American Letters of a Japanese Parlor-Maid*, 1905），诗集《自东海而来》（*From the Eastern*

Sea, 1903)、《夏云》(*The Summer Cloud*, 1906)以及有关日本诗歌、艺术的著作《日本诗歌的精神》(*The Spirit of Japanese Poetry*, 1914)、《日本艺术的精神》(*The Spirit of Japanese Art*, 1914)和自传性作品《野口米次郎的故事》(*The Story of Yone Noguchi*, 1915)等。野口米次郎被誉为"现代主义诗歌的先驱",也被认为是一个跨文化、跨国或国际化的作家。最近,野口的作品受到了美国亚裔文学研究者的关注。

《日本女孩的美国日记》这本书描述了牵牛花(Morning Glory)和叔叔进行横贯美国大陆之旅时的准备工作、活动和观察。他们乘蒸汽船抵达旧金山,牵牛花短暂地接管经营一家雪茄店。之后,他们搬到了奥克兰一位名叫海涅(Heine)的当地古怪诗人的乡村住宅。在那里度过了几天的时间之后,又去洛杉矶进行短暂的旅行。之后,她和叔叔离开美国西海岸前往芝加哥和纽约,一路上继续对美国生活和文化的各个方面进行讽刺观察。在小说的结尾,牵牛花公开表示,她打算通过做一份家仆的工作来继续调查美国人的生活。下文节选部分为本书的第二部分,讲述了作者在跨越大洋前往美国的航程中的所感、所想。

作品选读

The American Diary of a Japanese Girl

On the Ocean

"BELGIC," 7th

Good-night——native land!
Farewell, beloved Empress of Dai Nippon!

12th—The tossing spectacle of the waters (also the hostile smell of the ship) put my head in a whirl before the "Belgic" left the wharf.

The last five days have been a continuous nightmare. How many a time would I have preferred death!

My little self wholly exhausted by sea-sickness. Have I to drift to America in skin and bone?

I felt like a paper flag thrown in a tempest.

The human being is a ridiculously small piece. Nature plays with it and kills it when she pleases.

I cannot blame Balboa for his fancy, because he caught his first view from the peak in Darien.

It's not the "Pacifc Ocean." The breaker of the world!

"Do you feel any better?" inquired my fellow passenger.

He is the new minister to the City of Mexico on his way to his post. My uncle is one of his closest friends.

What if Meriken ladies should mistake me for the "sweet" wife of such a shabby pock-marked gentleman?

It will be all right, I thought, for we shall part at San Francisco.

(The pock-mark is rare in America, Uncle said. No country has a special demand for it, I suppose.)

His boyish carelessness and samurai-fashioned courtesy are characteristic. His great laugh, "Ha, ha, ha!" echoes on half a mile.

He never leaves his wine glass alone. My uncle complains of his empty stomach.

The more the minister repeats his cup the more his eloquence rises on the Chinese question. He does not forget to keep up his honourable standard of diplomatist even in drinking, I fancy.

I see charm in the eloquence of a drunkard.

I exposed myself on deck for the first time.

I wasn't strong enough, alas! to face the threatening grandeur of the ocean. Its divineness struck and wounded me.

O such an expanse of oily-looking waters! O such a menacing largeness!

One star, just one sad star, shone above.

I thought that the little star was trembling alone on a deck of some ship in the sky.

Star and I cried.

13th—My first laughter on the ocean burst out while I was peeping at a label, "7 yens," inside the chimney-pot hat of our respected minister, when he was brushing it.

He must have bought that great headgear just on the eve of his appointment.

How stupid to leave such a bit of paper!

I laughed.

He asked what was so irresistibly funny.

I laughed more. I hardly repressed "My dear old man."

The "helpless me" clinging on the bed for many a day feels splendid to-day.

The ocean grew placid.

On the land my eyes meet with a thousand temptations. They are here opened for nothing but the waters or the sun-rays.

I don't gain any lesson, but I have learned to appreciate the demonstrations of light.

They were white. O what a heavenly whiteness!

The billows sang a grand slow song in blessing of the sun, sparkling their ivory teeth.

The voyage isn't bad, is it?

I planted myself on the open deck, facing Japan.

I am a mountain-worshipper.

Alas! I could not see that imperial dome of snow, Mount Fuji.

One dozen fairies—two dozen—roved down from the sky to the ocean.

I dreamed.

I was so very happy.

14th—What a confusion my hair has suffered! I haven't put it in order since I left the Orient. Such negligence of toilet would be fined by the police in Japan.

I was busy with my hair all the morning.

15th—The Sunday service was held.

There's nothing more natural on a voyage than to pray.

We have abandoned the land. The ocean has no bottom.

We die any moment "with bubbling groan, without a grave, unknelled, uncoffined, and unknown."

Only prayer makes us firm.

I addressed myself to the Great Invisible whose shadow lies across my heart.

He may not be the ... of Christianity. He is not the Hotoke Sama of Buddhism.

Why don't those red-faced sailors hum heavenly-voiced hymns instead of—"swear?"

16th—Amerikey is away beyond.

Not even a speck of San Francisco in sight yet!

I amused myself thinking what would happen if I never returned home.

Marriage with a 'Merican, wealthy and comely?

I had wellnigh decided that I would not cross such an ocean again by ship. I would wait patiently until a trans-Pacific railroad is erected.

I was basking in the sun.

I fancied the "Belgic" navigating a wrong track.

What then?

Was I approaching lantern-eyed demons or howling cannibals?

"Iya, iya, no! I will proudly land on the historical island of Lotos Eaters," I said.

Why didn't I take Homer with me? The ocean is just the place for his majestic simplicity and lofty swing.

I recalled a few passages of "The Lotos Eaters" by Lord Tennyson—it sounds better than "the poet Tennyson." I love titles, but they are thought as common as millionaires nowadays.

A Jap poet has a different mode of speech.

Shall I pose as poet?

'Tis no great crime to do so.

I began my "Lotos Eaters" with the following mighty lines:

"O dreamy land of stealing shadows!

O peace-breathing land of calm afternoon!

O languid land of smile and lullaby!

O land of fragrant bliss and flower!

O eternal land of whispering Lotos Eaters!"

Then I feared that some impertinent poet might have said the same thing many a year before.

Poem manufacture is a slow job.

Modern people slight it, calling it an old fashion. Shall I give it up for some more brilliant up-to-date pose?

17th—I began to knit a gentleman's stockings in wool.

They will be a souvenir of this voyage.

(I cannot keep a secret.)

I tell you frankly that I designed them to be given to the gentleman who will be my future "beloved."

The wool is red, a symbol of my sanguine attachment.

The stockings cannot be much larger than my own feet. I dislike large-footed gentlemen.

18th—My uncle asked if my great work of poetical inspiration was completed.

"Uncle, I haven't written a dozen lines yet. My 'Lotos Eaters' is to be equal in length to 'The Lady of the Lake.' Now, see, Oji San, mine has to be far superior to the laureate's, not merely in quality, but in quantity as well. But I thought it was not the way of a sweet Japanese girl to plunder a garland from the old poet by writing in rivalry. Such a nice man Tennyson was!" I said.

I smiled and gazed on him slyly.

"So! You are very kind!" he jerked.

19th—I don't think San Francisco is very far off now. Shall I step out of the ship and walk?

Has the "Belgic" coal enough? I wonder how the sensible steamer can be so slow.

Let the blank pages pass quickly! Let me come face to face with the new chapter—"America!"

The gray monotone of life makes me insane. Such an eternal absence of variety on the ocean!

20th—The moon—how large is the ocean moon! —sat above my head.

When I thought that that moon must have been visiting in my dearest home of Tokio, the tragic scene of my "Sayonara, mother!" instantly returned.

Tears on my cheeks!

Morning, 21st—Three P. M. of to-day!

At last!

Beautiful Miss Morning Glory shall land on her dream-land, Amerikey.

That's my humble name, sir.

18 years old.

(Why does the 'Merican lady regard it as an insult to be asked her own age?)

My knitting work wasn't half done. I look upon it as an omen that I shall have no luck in meeting with my husband.

Tsumaranai! What a barren life!

Our great minister was placing a button on his shirt. His trembling fingers were uncertain.

I snatched the shirt from his hand and exhibited my craft with the needle.

"I fancied that you modern girls were perfect strangers to the needle," he said.

He is not blockish, I thought, since he permits himself to employ irony.

My uncle was lamenting that he had not even one cigar left.

Both those gentlemen offered to help me in my dressing at the landing.

I declined gracefully.

Where is my looking-glass?

I must present myself very—very pretty.

4

(Kazuo Miyamoto, 1897—1988)
宫本和男

作者简介

宫本和男（Kazuo Miyamoto, 1897—1988）出生于夏威夷的奥奥卡拉（O'okala, Hawaii），家中还有两个兄弟和三个姐妹。宫本曾就读于斯坦福大学，并在密苏里州圣路易斯的华盛顿大学医学院学习医学。在第二次世界大战期间，宫本被辗转拘押监禁于夏威夷和美国本土多地，最终同夏威夷群岛的众多日裔一道被拘押在沙岛（Sand Island）。在此期间，他开始写作《夏威夷：彩虹的尽头》（*Hawaii: End of the Rainbow*），历时 17 载才完成。

小说的第一部分主要讲述了两个一世家族——新田（Arata）和村山（Murayama）家族——离开日本到考艾岛（Kauai）和夏威夷的种植园工作时的经历。宫本描绘了日本劳工在艰苦的条件下从事田间工作或在种植园的磨坊里劳作时所面临的各种挑战。在站稳脚跟之后，大量的"照片新娘"来到夏威夷，日裔一世们开始建立新生的日本社区。小说第二部分主要讲述了二世日裔的生活。随着日裔成功地美国化，在日本和美国两国之间敌对情绪日益加剧的情况下，一些二世日裔为了获得更好的工作和教育机会仍然前往并定居在美国本土。小说的第三部分主要讲述了第二次世界大战期间新田和村山两家人被强制拘押的经历。在被转移到不同的拘留营后，命运的转折使他们在阿肯色州的杰罗姆重新团聚。随着战争的结束，新田和村山两个家庭被允许返回夏威夷的家园，开始重建生活。

节选为本书的第 29 章，叙述日裔被强制迁往图利湖（Tule Lake）拘留营的经历。

作品选读

Hawaii: End of the Rainbow

Tule Lake Relocation Center
(Excerpt)

"WHAT A PLACE! WHY, THERE Is NOTHING in the room but iron beds, mattresses and old blankets," dejectedly said Robert as he sat down on the iron cot as soon as he entered the assigned apartment in Block 6. The other members of the family looked about the bare walls of the twenty by twent-five foot room. The floor was littered with lumber and shavings. Everywhere a layer of fine dust and sand covered the surface. There was a large pig iron stove in the center of the room with a chimney straight up through the roof. This heating device reminded them that in the winter the temperature was going to descend much more than at Sacramento.

Minoru Murayama looked out of the window which was six-paned and slid lateralwise to shut out the cold and sand. The construction of this center had been rushed day and night to meet a deadline and there was neither time nor manpower to tidy up the area. The rear of the barrack that confronted him was littered with odds and ends of lumber and tar paper that were used to cover the walls and roof. He had just arrived with his family among a group of vanguard workers from the Sacramento area to prepare this small city to receive the thousands of evacuees from Northern California, Oregon, and Washington that were to follow in a few weeks. A similar group of workers had arrived from the State of Washington about a week earlier and they had already begun organization work.

When the Sacramento train pulled into the railroad siding, trucks operated by the Washington men transported the new arrivals to a large warehouse in which desks and chairs were installed and young women from the north processed the families from California. The family was the unit, designated by a number. Each member was photographed, like criminals for the rogues' gallery, and fingerprinted.

In war time and for an emergency undertaking, such humiliating treatment could perhaps be condoned, but just the same there was a turbulent resentment in everyone's heart. To be uprooted on short notice, labeled as a security risk just because of racial extraction, and now herded together in this bleak camp for the duration of the war, irrespective of how loyal a citizen may be to the country of his birth, was a fact not altogether easy to swallow. It might have been more gracefully accepted had other Americans of German and Italian descent been similarly treated as a war measure.

Evacuation from coastal areas of the Pacific slope for a distance of one hundred miles was imposed only on Japanese, irrespective of citizenship. The galling content of this edict lay in the realization that the governing body had no trust in Japanese-American citizens who were far more Americanized than was realized by the policy makers of the nation who were sorrowfully deficient in the knowledge of what Americanization had accomplished, not only among the native born group, but even among the aliens that had found the American way of life preferable to the age-long habits handed down from their ancestors from time immemorial. "Once a Jap, always a Jap," so had General De Witt stigmatized the persons of Japanese ancestry and put into motion an unprecedented mass evacuation of a race.

This movement could be compared to the displacement of the farmers of the Ukraine or Caucasus to the communes of Siberia by Soviet Russia. One less bitterly critical could find solace in discovering a counterpart in the romantic account of Longfellow's *Evangeline*: the tragic forced emigration of the French settlers of Arcadia in Canada to Louisiana Territory. The former was condemned as brutality that could only be carried out by inhuman communist dictators, and the latter an inhumanity against fellow minorities prepared in the garb of sentimentality and romance to induce copious sympathetic tears of the adolescent, but the only difference was of scope and magnitude.

How historians would interpret this emergency measure and hysterical outburst against a helpless minority Minoru speculated, for eventually it had to be evaluated by more balanced and trained individuals in a more stabilized era, for such critical analysis constituted the backbone of American democracy. Like any society of peoples, America was full of crooked politicians and unscrupulous rascals in government places, but democracy was courageous enough to clear house in sober moments.

Be that as it may, Minoru was now mentally re-enacting the scene at the Sacramento Station when family after family was transported on military trucks, disgorged onto the platform with just handbags of clothing and boxes of minimum daily necessities. Forlornly waiting for the arrival of the remainder of the contingent that were to make up this vanguard unit, they presented a sorry spectacle. There were the aged and the sick and the maimed. The military was merciful in that it adhered to the rule: keep family members together as a unit. They sat on their luggage and boxes while the young and restless paced the platform.

Expressions of resentment were conspicuously absent; days of anger were past. Now there was complete resignation and they acted as automatons, like sheep driven to the market for slaughter. Where they were destined to be transported nobody knew. It was a "military secret."

The non-commissioned officers and enlisted men of the military police were kind and helpful, assisting the women and the aged in alighting from the high trucks. Nevertheless, they were armed. With military punctuality the evacuees were brought to the station, counted, and loaded into the coaches. At the signal of a whistle, without fanfare and without anyone seeing them off, they left their homes behind.

The train headed north through the fat fertile farmland, crossing rivers, wheatland, and orchards. It wound and climbed its way among giant sequoias and pine trees to the plateau of the Oregon border. It traversed grazing land and finally crossed a lava-strewn district and came to their destination. The bare mountain to the left was no higher than a hill; only the proximity made it appear imposing. To the right in a vast compact area was an unmistakable town. There were rows and rows of black barracks in a bleak setting of desert land and in the distance, on a higher elevation, a solitary mountain shaped like an abalone stood like a landmark. There were high fences around the area with watch towers. The name of this camp was Tule Lake Center.

June the Second in Sacramento was already full summer and it was hot, but at this elevation of five thousand feet the evening was comfortably chilly. From a nearby hall metallic clanging resounded and without being told everyone knew that it was a summons to supper. Having nothing else to do the Murayama family of seven stood up to go to the mess hall.

In the course of twelve years, after completion of internship at Omaha, Minoru had married a girl born and raised in Sacramento and they had three children: Mary, Robert, and Russel. Both of his parents were still healthy. No longer did they toil on the delta farm, but lived with their eldest son. The other children had left home to begin their life in the vicinity of the capital of California.

The dining hall was a huge place and built to accommodate two hundred and fifty people, roughly the number that were to reside in each block. Cafeteria style serving was done and each had his tray loaded with sausage, sauerkraut, potatoes, bread pudding, and bread with oleomargarine. It was appetizing and each found that he was hungry after the long hours of jolting in the springless railway coach. When the early diners were finished an intelligent looking young man appeared and spoke to the assembly.

"My name is Kubo. I'm from the Puyallup Center and formerly from Seattle, Washington. Welcome to the Tule Lake War Relocation Center. We have been here a week trying to get this center organized. As you have seen since your arrival, everything has to be done from scratch. You from Northern California and Oregon will have to help us get this place organized to receive the bulk of the evacuees who will follow in two weeks. About five hundred of you have arrived today and you will choose or be chanelled into the type of work you are trained for or want to get a crack at. Being a community of people, the usual kind of work necessary in the daily lives of any society will be found here. You will be assigned to any type of work, but it will not be free enterprise like on the outside. The WRA will pay twelve, sixteen, and nineteen dollars a month plus clothing allowance... about three dollars per person.

5
(Toshio Mori, 1910—1980)
森敏雄

作者简介

  森敏雄（Toshio Mori，1910—1980）是成名最早的美国日裔二世作家。他出生于加州奥克兰，父母是经由夏威夷移民到美国西海岸定居的一世日本移民。青年时期，森敏雄喜欢文学，阅读了大量的文学作品，并立志成为一名作家。为此，他白天在自家经营的苗圃里辛勤工作以养家糊口，夜晚抽出时间写作。这个时期他笔耕不辍，写了很多短篇小说，但是基本没有发表。直到1938年，森敏雄才发表自己的第一部短篇小说《兄弟》（*The Brothers*），从此他的作品开始出现在日裔报刊以及美国一些主流刊物上。当时，著名作家威廉·索洛因（William Saroyan）对他的小说很欣赏，二人成为好友。也正是在索洛因的推荐下，一家小出版社计划在1942年出版森敏雄的小说集《加州横滨》（*Yokohama, California*）。但是太平洋战争的爆发以及随后而来的日裔强制迁徙、拘禁不仅改变了森敏雄的生活，还打乱了这部小说集的出版计划。直到1949年，这部小说集才得以正式出版。在第二次世界大战期间，森敏雄和家人被关押在犹他州的托帕兹（Topaz）拘留营中，并负责编辑杂志《旅行》（*The Trek*）。第二次世界大战后，他回到旧金山湾区继续写作。《加州横滨》是美国第一部关于日裔的小说集，出版后受到好评，这本书确立了森敏雄美国日裔文学奠基人的地位。但是很快，小说集就绝版并不为人知了，直到1970年代后，它才重新被亚裔学者发掘出来并受到研究人员的重视。除《加州横滨》外，森敏雄已出版的作品还包括长篇小说《广岛来的女人》（*Woman from Hiroshima*, 1978）以及短篇小说集《沙文主义者和其他故事》（*The Chauvinist and Other Stories*, 1979）。

下文节选部分是《加州横滨》一书中的短篇小说《世界之蛋》("The Eggs of the World")。小说主人公早川都衣（Sessue Matoi）是一位以酗酒摆脱自我囚禁并尽力催促周围的人们从禁锢他们的"内部的壳"中摆脱出来的哲学家。早川认为，世人皆是为心中之墙所囚禁的囚徒，个人心中的这堵墙，或者说蛋壳只能从内部打破。因此，被束缚的个人必须依靠自身的努力获得自由和解放。尽管早川的生活一团糟，但是他感觉自己是"自由人"，因此不需要别人的怜悯。

作品选读

Yokohama, California

The Eggs of the World

ALMOST EVERYONE IN THE COMMUNITY KNEW SESSUE Matoi as the heavy drinker. There was seldom a time when one did not see him staggering full of drink. The trouble was that the people did not know when he was sober or drunk. He was very clever when he was drunk and also very clever when sober. The people were afraid to touch him. They were afraid of this man, sober or drunk, for his tongue and brains. They dared not coax him too solicitously or make him look ridiculous as they would treat the usual tipsy gentleman. The people may have had only contempt for him but they were afraid and silent. And Sessue Matoi did little work. We always said he practically lived on sake and wit. And that was not far from truth.

I was at Mr. Hasegawa's when Sessue Matoi staggered in the house with several drinks under his belt. About the only logical reason I could think of for his visit that night was that Sessue Matoi must have known that Mr. Hasegawa carried many bottles of Japan-imported sake. There was no other business why he should pay a visit to Hasegawa's. I knew Mr. Hasegawa did not tolerate drinking bouts. He disliked riotous scenes and people.

At first I thought Mr. Hasegawa might have been afraid of this drinker, and Sessue Matoi had taken advantage of it. But this was not the case. Mr. Hasegawa was not afraid of Sessue Matoi. As I sat between the two that night I knew I was in the fun, and as likely as any minute something would explode.

"I came to see you on a very important matter, Hasegawa," Sessue Matoi said without batting an eye. "You are in a very dangerous position. You will lose your life."

"What are you talking about?" Mr. Hasegawa said.

"You are in an egg," Sessue Matoi said. "You have seen nothing but the inside of an egg and I feel sorry for you. I pity you."

"What are you talking about? Are you crazy?" Mr. Hasegawa said.

"I am not crazy. I see you very clearly in an egg," Sessue Matoi said. "That is very bad. Pretty soon you will be rotten."

Mr. Hasegawa was a serious fellow, not taking to laughter and gaiety. But he laughed out loud. This was ridiculous. Then he remembered Sessue Matoi was drunk.

"What about this young fellow?" Mr. Hasegawa said, pointing at me.

Sessue Matoi looked me over quizzically. He appeared to study me from all angles. Then he said, "His egg is forming. Pretty soon he must break the shell of his egg or little later will find himself too weak to do anything about it."

I said nothing. Mr. Hasegawa sat with a twinkle in his eyes.

"What about yourself, Sessue Matoi?" he said. "Do you live in an egg?"

"No," Sessue Matoi said. "An egg is when you are walled in, a prisoner within yourself. I am free, I have broken the egg long ago. You see as I am. I am not hidden beneath a shell and I am not enclosed in one either. I am walking on this earth with my good feet, and also I am drinking and enjoying, but am sad on seeing so many eggs in the world, unbroken, untasted, and rotten."

"Are you insulting the whole world or are you just insulting me?" Mr. Hasegawa said.

"I am insulting no one. Look, look me in the eye, Hasegawa. See how sober I am," he said. "I am not insulting you. I love you. I love the whole world and sober or drunk it doesn't make a bit of difference. But when I say an egg's an egg I mean it. You can't very well break the eggs I see."

"Couldn't you break the eggs for us?" Mr. Hasegawa said. "You seem to see the eggs very well. Couldn't you go around and break the shells and make this world the hatching ground?"

"No, no!" Sessue Matoi said. "You have me wrong! I cannot break the eggs. You cannot break the eggs. You can break an egg though."

"I don't get you," said Mr. Hasegawa.

"An egg is broken from within," said Sessue Matoi. "The shell of an egg melts by itself through heat or warmth and it's natural, and independent."

"This is ridiculous," said Mr. Hasegawa. "An egg can be broken from outside. You know very well an egg may be broken by a rap from outside."

"You can rape and assault too," said Sessue Matoi.

"This is getting to be fantastic," Mr. Hasegawa said. "This is silly! Here we are getting all burned up over a little egg, arguing over nonsense."

"This is very important to me," Sessue Matoi said. "Probably the only thing I know about. I study egg culture twenty-four hours. I live for it."

"And for sake," Mr. Hasegawa said.

"And for sake," Sessue Matoi said.

"Shall we study about sake tonight? Shall we taste the sake and you tell me about the flavor?" Mr. Hasegawa said.

"Fine, fine, fine!" said Mr. Matoi.

Mr. Hasegawa went back in the kitchen and we heard him moving about. Pretty soon he came back with a steaming bottle of sake. "This is Hakushika," he said.

"Fine, fine," Sessue Matoi said. "All brands are the same to me, all flavors match my favor. When I drink I am drinking my flavor."

Mr. Hasegawa poured him several cups which Sessue Matoi promptly gulped down. Sessue Matoi gulped down several more.

"Ah, when I drink sake I think of the eggs in the world," he said. "All the unopened eggs in the world."

"Just what are you going to do with all these eggs lying about? Aren't you going to do something about it? Can't you put some of the eggs aside and heat them up or warm them and help break the shells from within?" Mr. Hasegawa said.

"No," Sessue Matoi said. "I am doing nothing of the sort. If I do all you think I should do, then I will have no time to sit and drink. And I must drink. I cannot go a day without drinking because when I drink I am really going outward, not exactly drinking but expressing myself outwardly, talking very much and saying little, sadly and pathetically."

"Tell me, Sessue Matoi," said Mr. Hasegawa. "Are you sad at this moment? Aren't you happy in your paganistic fashion, drinking and laughing through twenty-four hours?"

"Now, you are feeling sorry for me, Hasegawa," Sessue Matoi said. "You are getting sentimental. Don't think of me in that manner. Think of me as the mess I am. I am a mess. Then laugh very hard, keep laughing very hard. Say, oh what an egg he has opened up! Look at the shells, look at the drunk without a bottle."

"Why do you say these things?" Mr. Hasegawa said. "You are very bitter."

"I am not bitter, I am not mad at anyone," Sessue Matoi said. "But you are still talking through the eggshell."

"You are insulting me again," Mr. Hasegawa said. "Do not allow an egg to come between us."

"That is very absurd," Sessue Matoi said, rising from his chair. "You are very absurd, sir. An egg is the most important and the most disturbing thing in the world. Since you are an egg, you do not know an egg. That is sad. I say, good night, gentlemen."

Sessue Matoi in all seriousness bowed formally and then tottered to the door.

"Wait, Sessue Matoi," said Mr. Hasegawa. "You didn't tell me what you thought of the flavor of my sake."

"I did tell you," Sessue Matoi said. "I told you the flavor right along."

"That's the first time I ever heard you talking about the flavor of sake tonight," said Mr. Hasegawa.

"You misunderstand me again," said Sessue Matoi. "When you wish to taste the flavor of sake which I drank then you must drink the flavor which I have been spouting all evening. Again, good night, gentlemen."

Again he bowed formally at the door and staggered out of the house.

I was expecting to see Mr. Hasegawa burst out laughing the minute Sessue Matoi stepped out of the house. He didn't. "I suppose he will be around in several days to taste your sake. This must happen every time he comes to see you," I said.

"No," Mr. Hasegawa said. "Strangely, this is the first time he ever walked out like that. I cannot understand him. I don't believe he will be back for a long time."

"Was he drunk or sober tonight?" I said.

"I really don't know, said Mr. Hasegawa. "He must be sober and drunk at the same time."

"Do you really think we will not see him for awhile?" I said.

"Yes, I am very sure of it. To think that an egg would come between us!"

6

(Miné Okubo, 1912—2001)
梅内·大久保

作者简介

梅内·大久保（Miné Okubo，1912—2001）是著名美国日裔作家、艺术家。梅内出生于加利福尼亚州，并于1938年获得加州大学伯克利分校美术硕士学位。之后两年的时间，梅内在法国和意大利旅行，继续自己的艺术之旅。1939到1942年，从欧洲回到美国后，在联邦艺术项目的委托下，她创作了几幅壁画。1942年，珍珠港事件后，她与自己的弟弟——在伯克利大学就读的学生大久保德（Toku Okubo）一道被转移到坦福兰（Tanforan）的美国日裔集合中心。那里的生活条件很差，他们住在经过改造的只有军用小床的马厩里，过着每天登记两次、宵禁和缺乏隐私的生活。6个月后，大久保和弟弟被转移到犹他州的托帕兹拘留营中。这期间梅内几乎从未离开她的素描本，记录她在拘留营中的生活。与此同时，她也帮助创办了托帕兹拘留营中的日裔文学杂志《旅行》。

离开拘留营之后，梅内在纽约定居，并出版了一部漫画小说《13660号公民》（*Citizen 13660*, 1946），讲述了她在加州和犹他州的拘留营中的生活经历。这部小说包含了近200张她用钢笔和墨水画的素描，并附有说明文字，记录了日本人和美国日裔被关押在拘留营中的生活。大久保认为自己的漫画小说是"第一部也是唯一一部由当时在场的人编写和绘图的日本人撤离和搬迁的纪录片"，她通过线条画和中性的叙述，为读者提供了一个独特的视角来看待美国日裔被关押的历史记录。

下文内容节选自梅内的小说《13660号公民》，主要叙述了美国日裔被强行拘禁迁徙至托帕兹拘留营中。在拘留营艰苦的条件下，日裔重建自己的家庭、生活。之后，部分年轻人被允许离开拘留营，前往美国中东部地区学习、工作。

作品选读

Citizen 13660

(Excerpt)

THE program of segregation was now instituted. One of its purposes was to protect loyal Japanese Americans from the continuing threats of pro-Japanese agitators. Tule Lake, one of the ten original centers, was chosen as the segregation center for the disloyal. In the fall of 1943 thirteen hundred Topazians (about one tenth of the total) were sent there. The group included all who had said they wished to return to Japan; the "No, nos," that is, those who would not change their unsatisfactory answers to the questionnaire when they were given a chance to do so; all who remained under suspicion of disloyalty after investigation by the War Relocation Authority and the Federal Bureau of Investigation; and close relatives who would rather be segregated with their families than be separated from them.

Whatever decision was made, families suffered deeply. Children had to go to Tule Lake with their parents, but some adolescents resented the label "disloyal" and fought bitterly to remain behind.

TWELVE hundred loyal citizens and aliens were transferred from Tule Lake to Topaz. Their arrival once more brought excitement to our now relatively peaceful city.

THE rules were becoming much less rigid. Block shopping was introduced, whereby a resident of each block was permitted to shop in the nearby town of Delta for the rest of the block. Special permits were arranged ahead of time by the administration. There was a thorough inspection by the military police both on leaving and returning.

UNDER the change in rules, many now went outside the fences to the outer project area to gather vegetation and small stones for their gardens. Others hunted for arrow heads.

MANY went fishing in the irrigation ditches, about three miles away on the outskirts of the project's agricultural area.

RELOCATION programs were finally set up in the center to return residents to normal life. Students had led the way by going out to continue their education in the colleges and universities willing to accept them. Seasonal workers followed, to relieve the farm labor shortage.

Many volunteered for the army. Government jobs opened up, and the defense plants claimed others. The Intelligence Division of the army and navy demanded still others as instructors and students. My brother had left in June to work in a wax-paper factory in Chicago. Later he was inducted into the army.

Much red tape was involved, and "relocatees" were checked and double checked and rechecked. Citizens were asked to swear unqualified allegiance to the United States and to defend it faithfully from all foreign powers. Aliens were asked to swear to abide by the laws of the United States and to do nothing to interfere with the war effort. Jobs were checked by the War Relocation offices and even the place of destination was investigated before an evacuee left.

In January of 1944, having finished my documentary sketches of camp life, I finally decided to leave.

AFTER plowing through the red tape, through the madness of packing again, I attended forums on "How to Make Friends" and "How to Behave in the Outside World."

I was photographed.

THE day of my departure arrived. I dashed to the block manager's office to turn in the blankets and other articles loaned to me, and went to the Administration Office to secure signatures on the various forms given me the day before. I received a train ticket and $25, plus $3 a day for meals while traveling; these were given to each person relocating on an indefinite permit. I received four typewritten cards to be filled out and returned after relocation, and a booklet, "When You Leave the Relocation Center," which I was to read on the train.

I dashed to the mess hall for a bite to eat, then to the Administration Office, picked up my pass and ration book at the Internal Security Office, and hurried to the gate. There I shook hands with the friends who had gathered to see me off. I lined up to be checked by the WRA and the army.

I was now free.

I looked at the crowd at the gate. Only the very old or very young were left. Here I was, alone, with no family responsibilities, and yet fear had chained me to the camp. I thought, "My...! How do they expect those poor people to leave the one place they can call home." I swallowed a lump in my throat as I waved goodbye to them.

I entered the bus. As soon as all the passengers had been accounted for, we were on our way. I relieved momentarily the sorrows and the joys of my whole evacuation experience, until the barracks faded away into the distance. There was only the desert now. My thoughts shifted from the past to the future.

7

(Monica Sone, 1919—2011)
莫妮卡·曾根

作者简介

  莫妮卡·曾根（Monica Sone，也译作莫妮卡·索恩，1919—2011），原名系井和子（Kazuko Itoi），出生于西雅图，父母是日本移民，在西雅图经营一家酒店。她同许多二世孩子一样，不仅学习美国课程，还学习日语和日本文化课程。1942年5月，曾根同家人一起从西雅图的家中被强制迁移至艾奥瓦州米尼多卡的拘留营（internment camp at Minidoka, Idaho）里。1943年，她被允许离开营地到芝加哥求学，在当地的汉诺威学院（Hanover College）获得了本科学位，并于1949年获得凯斯西储大学（Case Western Reserve University）临床心理学硕士学位。随后，她成为了天主教社区联盟的临床心理学家和社会工作者，从业38年。2011年，她在度过92岁生日后不久在坎顿（Canton, Ohio）去世。

  曾根的《二世女儿》（*Nisei Daughter*, 1953）被誉为20世纪上半期最成功的日裔文学作品。在书中，她用第一人称的形式叙述了其父母从日本移民到美国，历经各种磨难，最终通过自身的努力在美国站稳脚跟，并实现安居乐业的经历。这是一个典型的移民成功实现美国梦的故事，但是书中很重要的一部分是他们一家人在第二次世界大战期间被强制迁移关押到拘留营中的经历。本书出版于1953年，这个时期很多日裔为了向美国公众证明他们并非那些"不可同化的外国人"而对自己的集中营创伤经历三缄其口。因此，作者在叙述家人的拘留营经历时，并没有突出营中的艰难困苦，而是突出日裔的艰苦奋斗以及拘留营经历对日裔的所谓"正面作用"。

下文节选部分为本书第 11 章，故事的叙述者讲述自己离开拘留营后在芝加哥的工作学习生活。

作品选读

Nisei Daughter

Chapter XI

Eastward, Nisei

(Excerpt)

BY 1943, scarcely a year after Evacuation Day, the War Relocation Authority was opening channels through which the Nisei could return to the main stream of life. It granted permanent leave to anyone cleared by the FBI who had proof of a job and a place to live. Students were also released if they had been accepted into colleges and universities.

The West Coast was still off-limits, but we had access to the rest of the continent where we could start all over again. The Midwest and East suddenly loomed before us, an exciting challenge. Up till then America for me had meant the lovely city of Seattle, a small Japanese community and a desperate struggle to be just myself. Now that I had shed my past, I hoped that I might come to know another aspect of America which would inject strength into my hyphenated Americanism instead of pulling it apart.

Matsuko, my childhood friend, was one of the first to leave camp. Through a church program, the Reverend Mr. and Mrs. W. Trumble of Chicago had become interested in helping individual evacuees. They had written Matsuko, telling her about a job as a stenographer in a large department store and inviting her to live with them. From Chicago, Matsuko deluged me with enthusiastic letters, telling me what wonderful folks the Trumbles were and how happy she was with her job. She said she no longer felt self-conscious about her Oriental face and that she was breathing free and easy for the first time in her life. Matsuko urged me to leave Minidoka and spoke to the Trumbles about me. One day I received a cordial letter from a Dr. and Mrs.

John Richardson. Dr. Richardson was a pastor at a Presbyterian Church in a suburb of Chicago. He told me of a dentist, desperately in need of an assistant, who was willing to hire a Nisei. I was to live with the Richardsons.

I accepted Dr. Richardson's invitation posthaste, feeling as if it were a dream too good to be true. Father and Mother, although reluctant to see me go, accepted my decision to leave as part of the sadness which goes with bearing children who grow up and must be independent.

So when it was early in spring and the snow had thawed, I boarded a train in Shoshone, numbed with excitement and anxiety. For two days and two nights I remained wide-eyed and glued to my seat as we rushed headlong across the great continent. We finally hit Chicago, and I felt helpless in the giant, roaring metropolis, with its thundering vitality, perpetual wind and clouds of smoke. Hundreds of people and cars seemed to be rushing at each other at suicide speed. I was relieved to see that they were much too busy to notice the evacuees who had crept into town. I plunged and swam through this heaving mass of humanity until I found a taxi.

The Richardson residence was a large, two-story brown frame house in the suburbs. I pressed the doorbell with a nervous cold finger. A small woman with a beautiful halo of white hair and gentle gray eyes greeted me warmly. "Come in, Monica, I'm Mrs. Richardson. My husband and I've been expecting you. Here, let me help you with your suitcase." Her quiet, gracious manner disarmed me completely.

Dr. Richardson came out of his study, beaming. He was a great oak of a man, tall and solidly built. The rugged cut of his features, his deep vibrant voice, everything about him revealed a personality of strong purpose and will. He shook my hand so vigorously I felt like a tiny wren swaying on the end of a swinging branch.

"We're so glad to see you, Monica, so very glad," he said. "I hope you'll like it here."

I learned that the Richardsons had been China missionaries for many years. Mrs. Richardson brought out pictures of her sons, all three in the armed services: Gordon, the physician, in the army; Paul, in the navy; and John, the youngest, also in the army, somewhere in the Pacific. It was a curious sensation to be talking to these folks who knew and loved so much about China, a nation at war so long with Japan. I felt even stranger when I learned that Paul, the second son, was learning Japanese in naval intelligence. Eventually he would go out to meet his Japanese enemy, and John had probably already encountered them. Our entire relationship was interwoven in the grim business of war, and yet the Richardsons made me feel from the start that we were friends, that we had something in common, something which had nothing to do with politics, war and hate.

After we had chatted a while, Dr. Richardson remembered he had a call to make, and clapping on his hat and overcoat, he rushed out, telling me to make myself at home now that I *was* home.

Mrs. Richardson led me upstairs into an attractive, modestly furnished room. "This is yours, Monica. It was John, Jr.'s before he left for the army. I've emptied the closet and drawers so you may use them as you wish."

Mrs. Richardson walked to the window overlooking the spacious back yard and opened it slightly. A spring breeze wafted through the freshly starched curtain, bringing into the room the cool freshness of the trees, the lawn and the flower garden below. There was serenity and peace in this house which I knew was the reflection of this gentle woman's character.

"I'll go away now and let you rest," she said. "When you're ready, come downstairs for supper."

I stood alone in the room, very close to tears. It seemed as if I had at last come to the end of a long journey, and walked into a resting place for tired souls. I lay on the bed, weary, with the comfortable weariness which comes after release from tension. It was wonderful to have a room of my own again. I even had an elm tree of my own, towering right outside the south window, which broke the sunlight pouring into my room into a cool, shadowy pattern of dark-green leaves. There was a yellow bowl filled with fresh-cut flowers placed on the dresser. And I noticed that the night table standing beside my bed was covered with a Chinese scarf, a beautiful piece of rich blue satin, the intricate flowered design hand-embroidered with gold, carmine, jade green and purple threads. Mrs. Richardson must have placed it there for my enjoyment. I settled into my pillow with a warm feeling. I knew that I would become terribly lonely for my family now and then, but its sharpness would be dulled in this home, for here there was kindness and love, deep and unshakable. Tomorrow I would be able to write a gay letter to Father and Mother, telling them about my new friends.

In the beginning I worried a great deal about people's reactions to me. Before I left Camp Minidoka, I had been warned over and over again that once I was outside, I must behave as inconspicuously as possible so as not to offend the sensitive public eye. I made up my mind to make myself scarce and invisible, but I discovered that an Oriental face, being somewhat of a rarity in the Midwest, made people stop in their tracks, stare, follow and question me. At first I was dismayed with such attention, but I learned that it was out of curiosity and not hostility that they stared.

Much of the time people mistook me for Chinese, and they told me how well they thought of the Chinese, who were our allies, and what a dynamic personality Madame Chiang Kai-shek was. Once in a department store, a young wide-eyed salesgirl fluttered up to me, "May I have your autograph, Miss Wong?" I regretfully told her I was not Miss Wong, but for a fleeting second I felt the vicarious thrill of a celebrity. The young clerk had been thinking of Miss Anna May Wong who was in the same department store that day demonstrating cosmetics.

On another occasion, I was mistaken for Ming Toy, a Chinese fan dancer. As I stood waiting for a bus on a corner, a strange man dashed across the street, grinning widely and waving his hand at me. He came up, all graciousness.

"Good afternoon, Miss Toy! Er, ah, you are Miss Toy?"

I was confused for a moment. My name was "Itoi" and many times people dropped the first letter and simply called me "Miss Toy." I said, "Yes," hesitantly, wondering what this was leading up to. The man brightened. "Well, Miss Toy, I thought your number pretty snappy. How about lunch so we can talk about booking you at our cabaret. We can use a fan dancer now."

My jaws dropped, and I was unable to find words to express my shock. I flagged down an empty taxicab and dashed away, followed by the bewildered man who shouted after me, "Just a moment, Miss Toy! You are the fan dancer, aren't you?" People stopped to watch Ming Toy, the fan dancer, dive into a taxi.

8

(Hisaye Yamamoto, 1921—2011)
山本久枝

作者简介

  山本久枝（Hisaye Yamamoto，1921—2011）是美国日裔作家中重要的短篇小说家之一。她出生于加州雷东多海滩（Redondo Beach, California），父母是来自日本的一世移民。同许多日本移民一样，她的父母怀抱着梦想来到美国，但因为他们并非美国公民，因而无法拥有土地，只能成为流动季节工人，辗转于各地的农场谋生。山本的成长轨迹同其他日裔儿童没有太大区别，既读美国的公立学校，也参加日本语言学校，学习日本语言文化。山本喜欢阅读、写作，少年时代即开始向日语刊物的英文版投稿。太平洋战争爆发后，山本与家人一道被关入亚利桑那州的拘留营。在拘留营中，山本仍然坚持写作，作品发表在拘留营的内部刊物上。

  1945 年，离开拘留营后，山本曾在《洛杉矶论坛报》（*Los Angeles Tribune*）工作了一段时间。1948 年，她的《高跟鞋》（"The High-Heeled Shoes: A Memoir"）发表在主流刊物《党派评论》（*Partisan Review*）上，此后她开始陆续在全国性的刊物上发表小说。山本是一个多产的短篇小说家，陆陆续续发表了 61 篇作品。但是直到 1985 年才在日本出版一部包括 5 篇小说的小说集，1988 年美国一家出版社出版了她的英语版小说集《十七个音节》（*Seventeen Syllables*），包括 15 篇小说以及张敬珏教授的一篇前言。在这篇前言中，张敬珏教授概括了山本小说的主题 "……美国西部不同种族群体之间的互动关系，日本移民及其孩子之间的关系，以及一世在'新世界'里不愉快的适应过程，尤其是美国日裔妇女所遭受的种种限制"。实际上，山本除了叙述第二次世界大战之前日裔美国人在农场上的生活之外，日裔美国人在拘留营中的经历也是她创作的重要主题。

《褐色的房子》（"The Brown House"）是山本久枝创作于1951年的一篇短篇小说，探讨了陷入困境的妻子和种族互动的主题。服部先生（Hattori）为了弄点快钱而染上赌博的恶习。一次，他偶然发现一家隐藏的赌场，便谎称要进去办事，留下服部太太与孩子们在车里等待。整个下午他都在赌场里面，而里面的各色人等，包括黄种人、白种人以及黑人等等，都相安无事，融洽相处。警察来抓赌时，赌场中的赌客仓皇而逃，一个黑人慌不择路之下躲进了服部太太的车里，孩子们受到严重惊吓。故事的结尾黑人对服部太太表示感谢，并且认为日本人"洁净而又彬彬有礼"。

作品选读

The Brown House
(Excerpt)

In California that year the strawberries were marvelous. As large as teacups, they were so juicy and sweet that Mrs. Hattori, making her annual batch of jam, found she could cut down on the sugar considerably. "I suppose this is supposed to be the compensation," she said to her husband, whom she always politely called Mr. Hattori.

"Some compensation!" Mr. Hattori answered.

At that time they were still on the best of terms. It was only later, when the season ended as it had begun, with the market price for strawberries so low nobody bothered to pick number twos, that they began quarreling for the first time in their life together. What provoked the first quarrel and all the rest was that Mr. Hattori, seeing no future in strawberries, began casting around for a way to make some quick cash. Word somehow came to him that there was in a neighboring town a certain house where fortunes were made overnight, and he hurried there at the first opportunity.

It happened that Mrs. Hattori and all the little Hattoris, five of them, all boys and born about a year apart, were with him when he paid his first visit to the house. When he told them to wait in the car, saying he had a little business to transact inside and would return in a trice, he truly meant what he said. He intended only to give the place a brief inspection in order to familiarize himself with it. This was at two o'clock in the afternoon, however, and when he finally made his way back to the car, the day was already so dim that he had to grope around a bit for the door handle.

The house was a large but simple clapboard, recently painted brown and relieved with white window frames. It sat under several enormous eucalyptus trees in the foreground of a few acres of asparagus. To the rear of the house was a ramshackle barn whose spacious blue roof advertised in great yellow letters a ubiquitous brand of physic. Mrs. Hattori, peering toward the house with growing impatience, could not understand what was keeping her husband. She watched other cars either drive into the yard or park along the highway and she saw all sorts of people—white, yellow, brown, and black—enter the house. Seeing very few people leave, she got the idea that her husband was attending a meeting or a party.

So she was more curious than furious that first time when Mr. Hattori got around to returning to her and the children. To her rapid questions Mr. Hattori replied slowly, pensively: it was a gambling den run by a Chinese family under cover of asparagus, he said, and he had been winning at first, but his luck had suddenly turned, and that was why he had taken so long—he had been trying to win back his original stake at least.

"How much did you lose?" Mrs. Hattori asked dully.

"Twenty-five dollars," Mr. Hattori said.

"Twenty-five dollars!" exclaimed Mrs. Hattori. "Oh, Mr. Hattori, what have you done?"

At this, as though at a prearranged signal, the baby in her arms began wailing, and the four boys in the back seat began complaining of hunger. Mr. Hattori gritted his teeth and drove on. He told himself that this being assailed on all sides by bawling, whimpering, and murderous glances was no less than he deserved. Never again, he said to himself; he had learned his lesson.

Nevertheless, his car, with his wife and children in it, was parked near the brown house again the following week. This was because he had dreamed a repulsive dream in which a fat white snake had uncoiled and slithered about and everyone knows that a white-snake dream is a sure omen of good luck in games of chance. Even Mrs. Hattori knew this. Besides, she felt a little guilty about having nagged him so bitterly about the twenty-five dollars. So Mr. Hattori entered the brown house again on condition that he would return in a half hour, surely enough time to test the white snake. When he failed to return after an hour, Mrs. Hattori sent Joe, the oldest boy, to the front door to inquire after his father. A Chinese man came to open the door of the grille, looked at Joe, said, "Sorry, no kids in here," and clacked it to.

When Joe reported back to his mother, she sent him back again and this time a Chinese woman looked out and said, "What you want, boy?" When he asked for his father, she asked him to wait, then returned with him to the car, carrying a plate of Chinese cookies. Joe, munching one thick biscuit as he led her to the car, found its flavor and texture very strange; it was unlike either its American or Japanese counterpart so that he could not decide whether he liked it or not.

Although the woman was about Mrs. Hattori's age, she immediately called the latter "mama," assuring her that Mr. Hattori would be coming soon, very soon. Mrs. Hattori, mortified, gave excessive thanks for the cookies which she would just as soon have thrown in the woman's face. Mrs. Wu, for so she introduced herself, left them after wagging her head in amazement that Mrs. Hattori, so young, should have so many children and telling her frankly, "No wonder you so skinny, mama."

"Skinny, ha!" Mrs. Hattori said to the boys. "Well, perhaps. But I'd rather be skinny than fat."

Joe, looking at the comfortable figure of Mrs. Wu going up the steps of the brown house, agreed.

Again it was dark when Mr. Hattori came back to the car, but Mrs. Hattori did not say a word. Mr. Hattori made a feeble joke about the unreliability of snakes, but his wife made no attempt to smile. About halfway home she said abruptly, "Please stop the machine, Mr. Hattori. I don't want to ride another inch with you."

"Now, mother..." Mr. Hattori said. "I've learned my lesson. I swear this is the last time."

"Please stop the machine, Mr. Hattori," his wife repeated.

Of course the car kept going, so Mrs. Hattori, hugging the baby to herself with one arm, opened the door with her free hand and made as if to hop out of the moving car.

The car stopped with a lurch and Mr. Hattori, aghast, said, "Do you want to kill yourself?"

"That's a very good idea," Mrs. Hattori answered, one leg out of the door.

"Now, mother..." Mr. Hattori said. "I'm sorry; I was wrong to stay so long. I promise on my word of honor never to go near that house again. Come, let's go home now and get some supper."

"Supper!" said Mrs. Hattori. "Do you have any money for groceries?"

"I have enough for groceries," Mr. Hattori confessed.

Mrs. Hattori pulled her leg back in and pulled the door shut. "You see!" she cried triumphantly. "You see!"

The next time, Mrs. Wu brought out besides the cookies a paper sackful of Chinese firecrackers for the boys. "This is America," Mrs. Wu said to Mrs. Hattori. "China and Japan have war, all right, but (she shrugged) it's not our fault. You understand?"

Mrs. Hattori nodded, but she did not say anything because she did not feel her English up to the occasion.

"Never mind about the firecrackers or the war," she wanted to say. "Just inform Mr. Hattori that his family awaits without."

Suddenly Mrs. Wu, who out of the corner of her eye had been examining another car parked up the street, whispered, "Cops!" and ran back into the house as fast as she could carry her amplitude. Then the windows and doors of the brown house began to spew out all kinds of people—white, yellow, brown, and black—who either got into cars and drove frantically away or ran across the street to dive into the field of tall dry weeds. Before Mrs. Hattori and the boys knew what was happening, a Negro man opened the back door of their car and jumped in to crouch at the boys' feet.

The boys, who had never seen such a dark person at close range before, burst into terrified screams, and Mrs. Hattori began yelling too, telling the man to get out, get out. The panting man clasped his hands together and beseeched Mrs. Hattori, "Just let me hide in here until the police go away! I'm asking you to save me from jail!"

Mrs. Hattori made a quick decision. "All right," she said in her tortured English. "Go down, hide!" Then, in Japanese, she assured her sons that this man meant them no harm and ordered them to cease crying, to sit down, to behave, lest she be tempted to give them something to cry about. The policemen had been inside the house about fifteen minutes when Mr. Hattori came out. He had been thoroughly frightened, but now he managed to appear jaunty as he told his wife how he had cleverly thrust all incriminating evidence into a nearby vase of flowers and thus escaped arrest. "They searched me and told me I could go," he said. "A lot of others weren't so lucky. One lady fainted."

They were almost a mile from the brown house before the man in back said, "Thanks a million. You can let me off here."

Mr. Hattori was so surprised that the car screeched when it stopped. Mrs. Hattori hastily explained, and the man, pausing on his way out, searched for words to emphasize his gratitude. He had always been, he said, a friend of the Japanese people; he knew no race so cleanly, so well-mannered, so downright nice. As he slammed the door shut, he put his hand on the arm of Mr. Hattori, who was still dumfounded, and promised never to forget this act of kindness.

"What we got to remember," the man said, "is that we all got to die sometime. You might be a king in silk shirts or riding a white horse, but we all got to die sometime."

Mr. Hattori, starting up the car again, looked at his wife in reproach. "A *kurombo*!" he said. And again, "A *kurombo*!" He pretended to be victim to a shudder.

9

(Yoshiko Uchida, 1921—1992)
内田良子

作者简介

内田良子（Yoshiko Uchida, 1921—1992）出生于美国加州的阿拉梅达（Alameda, California），是美国著名儿童作家。1941年，正在加州大学伯克利分校就读的内田同家人被强制迁往犹他州的托帕兹拘留营。1943年，内田被马萨诸塞州的史密斯学院（Smith College in Massachusetts）录取，并获准离开拘留营，但那里的岁月给她留下了深刻的印象。内田作品的主题主要是有关种族、国籍、身份以及跨文化关系。她在1982年出版了自传《沙漠放逐》(*Desert Exile*)，书中内田用相当大的篇幅记述了自己的一世父母以及自己的拘留营经历。像其他有关拘留营书写的作品一样，内田在书中探讨了种族、身份以及由于放逐而造成的日裔心理问题。她的许多小说，如《照片新娘》(*Picture Bride*, 1987)和《手镯》(*The Bracelet*, 1976) 都是以日裔的眼光看待包括第一次世界大战、大萧条和第二次世界大战以及美国日裔遭受的种族主义歧视等历史事件的作品。内田还以儿童小说而闻名，主要有《跳舞的水壶和其他日本民间故事》(*Dancing Kettle and Other Japanese Folk Tales*, 1949)、《托帕兹之旅》(*Journey to Topaz*, 1971)、《金山武士》(*Samurai of Gold Hill*, 1971)、《回家之旅》(*Journey Home*, 1978) 以及《梦想的瓶子》(*A Jar of Dreams*, 1981) 等。

《照片新娘》这部小说讲述了日本女子花子（Hana）的故事。她是被包办婚姻带到美国的日本众多"照片新娘"之一。这部小说主要讲述了花子与丈夫太郎（Taro）以及女儿玛丽的关系。小说叙述了花子不得不通过包办婚姻来到美国，在美国系统性种族主义歧视中挣扎求生的故事。太平洋战争爆发后，花子一家的生活发生了剧烈动荡,他们被迫背井离乡,被关押在沙漠中的托帕兹拘留营中。虽然花子经历了悲剧的打击,但是她以自身顽强的精神和毅力在艰难的处境中生存下来。

节选部分为本书第一部分,叙述花子作为一名"照片新娘"离开祖国,远涉重洋到达美国一路上的见闻。

作品选读

Picture Bride

1

Hana Omiya stood at the railing of the small ship that shuddered toward America in a turbulent November sea. She shivered as she pulled the folds of her silk kimono close to her throat and tightened the wool shawl about her shoulders.

She was thin and small, her dark eyes shadowed in her pale face, her black hair piled high in a pompadour that seemed too heavy for so slight a woman. She clung to the moist rail and breathed the damp salt air deep into her lungs. Her body seemed leaden and lifeless, as though it were simply the vehicle transporting her soul to a strange new life, and she longed with childlike intensity to be home again in Oka Village.

She longed to see the bright persimmon dotting the barren trees beside the thatched roofs, to see the fields of golden rice stretching to the mountains where only last fall she had gathered plump white mushrooms, and to see once more the maple trees lacing their flaming colors through the green pine. If only she could see a familiar face, eat a meal without retching, walk on solid ground and stretch out at night on a tatami mat instead of in a hard narrow bunk. She thought now of seeking the warm shelter of her bunk but could not bear to face the relentless smell of fish that penetrated the lower decks.

Why did I ever leave Japan, she wondered bitterly. Why did I ever listen to my uncle? And yet she knew it was she herself who had begun the chain of events that placed her on this heaving ship. It was she who had first planted in her uncle's mind the thought that she would make a good wife for Taro Takeda, the lonely man who had gone to America to make his fortune in Oakland, California.

It all began one day when her uncle had come to visit her mother.

"I must find a nice young bride," he had said, startling Hana with this blunt talk of marriage in her presence. She blushed and was ready to leave the room when her uncle quickly added. "My good friend Takeda has a son in America. I must find someone willing to travel to that far land."

This last remark was intended to indicate to Hana and her mother that he didn't consider this a suitable prospect for Hana who was the youngest daughter of what once had been a fine family. Her father, until his death fifteen years ago, had been the largest landholder of the village and one of its last samurai. They had once had many servants and field hands, but now all that was changed. Their money was gone. Hana's three older sisters had made good marriages, and the eldest remained in their home with her husband to carry on the Omiya name and perpetuate the homestead. Her other sisters had married merchants in Osaka and Nagoya and were living comfortably.

Now that Hana was twenty-one, finding a proper husband for her had taken on an urgency that produced an embarrassing secretive air over the entire matter. Usually, her mother didn't speak of it until they were lying side by side on their quilts at night. Then, under the protective cover of darkness, she would suggest one name and then another, hoping that Hana would indicate an interest in one of them.

Her uncle spoke freely of Taro Takeda only because he was so sure Hana would never consider him. "He is a conscientious, hard-working man who has been in the United States for almost ten years. He is thirty-one, operates a small shop and rents some rooms above the shop where he lives." Her uncle rubbed his chin thoughtfully. "He could provide well for a wife," he added.

"Ah," Hana's mother said softly.

"You say he is successful in this business?" Hana's sister inquired.

"His father tells me he sells many things in his shop—clothing, stockings, needles, thread and buttons—such things as that. He also sells bean paste, pickled radish, bean cake and soy sauce. A wife of his would not go cold or hungry."

They all nodded, each of them picturing this merchant in varying degrees of success and affluence. There were many Japanese emigrating to America these days, and Hana had heard of the picture brides who went with nothing more than an exchange of photographs to bind them to a strange man.

"Taro San is lonely," her uncle continued. "I want to find for him a fine young woman who is strong and brave enough to cross the ocean alone."

"It would certainly be a different kind of life," Hana's sister ventured, and for a moment, Hana thought she glimpsed a longing ordinarily concealed behind her quiet, obedient face. In that same instant, Hana knew she wanted more for herself than her sisters had in their proper, arranged and loveless marriages. She wanted to escape the smothering strictures of life in her village. She certainly was not going to marry a farmer and spend her life working beside him planting, weeding and harvesting in the rice paddies until her back became bent from too many years of stooping and her skin turned to brown leather by the sun and wind. Neither did she particularly relish the idea of marrying a merchant in a big city as her two sisters had done. Since her mother objected to her going to Tokyo to seek employment as a teacher, perhaps she would consent to a flight to America for what seemed a proper and respectable marriage.

Almost before she realized what she was doing, she spoke to her uncle. "Oji San, perhaps I should go to America to make this lonely man a good wife."

"You, Hana Chan?" Her uncle observed her with startled curiosity. "You would go all alone to a foreign land so far away from your mother and family?"

"I would not allow it," Her mother spoke fiercely. Hana was her youngest and she had lavished upon her the attention and latitude that often befall the last child. How could she permit her to travel so far, even to marry the son of Takeda who was known to her brother.

But now, a notion that had seemed quite impossible a moment before was lodged in his receptive mind, and Hana's uncle grasped it with the pleasure that comes from an unexpected discovery.

"You know," he said, looking at Hana, "it might be a very good life in America."

Hana felt a faint fluttering in her heart. Perhaps this lonely man in America was her means of escaping both the village and the encirclement of her family.

Her uncle spoke with increasing enthusiasm of sending Hana to become Taro's wife. And the husband of Hana's sister, who was head of their household, spoke with equal eagerness. Although he never said so, Hana guessed he would be pleased to be rid of her, the spirited younger sister who stirred up his placid life with what he considered radical ideas about life and the role of women. He often claimed that Hana had too much schooling for a girl. She had graduated from Women's High School in Kyoto which gave her five more years of schooling than her older sister.

"It has addled her brain—all that learning from those books," he said when he tired of arguing with Hana.

A man's word carried much weight for Hana's mother. Pressed by the two men she consulted her other daughters and their husbands. She discussed the matter carefully with her brother and asked the village priest. Finally, she agreed to an exchange of family histories and an investigation was begun into Taro Takeda's family, his education and his health, so they would be assured there was no insanity or tuberculosis or police records concealed in his family's past. Soon Hana's uncle was devoting his energies entirely to serving as go-berween for Hana's mother and Taro Takeda's father.

When at last an agreement to the marriage was almost reached, Taro wrote his first letter to Hana. It was brief and proper and gave no more clue to his character than the stiff formal portrait taken at his graduation from Middle School. Hana's uncle had given her the picture with apologies from his parents because it was the only photo they had of him and it was not a flattering likeness.

Hana hid the letter and photograph in the sleeve of her kimono and took them to the outhouse to study in private. Squinting in the dim light and trying to ignore the foul odor, she read and reread Taro's letter, trying to find the real man somewhere in the sparse unbending prose.

By the time he sent her money for her steamship tickets, she had received ten more letters, but none revealed much more of the man than the first. In none did he disclose his loneliness or his need, but Hana understood this. In fact, she would have recoiled from a man who bared his intimate thoughts to her so soon. After all, they would have a lifetime together to get to know one another.

So it was that Hana had left her family and sailed alone to America with a small hope trembling inside of her. Tomorrow, at last, the ship would dock in San Francisco and she would meet face to face the man she was soon to marry. Hana was overcome with excitement at the thought of being in America and terrified of the meeting about to take place. What would she say to Taro Takeda when they first met, and for all the days and years after?

Hana wondered about the flat above the shop. Perhaps it would be luxuriously furnished with the finest of brocades and lacquers, and perhaps there would be a servant, although he had not mentioned it. She worried whether she would be able to manage on the meager English she had learned at Women's High School. The overwhelming anxiety for the day to come and the violent rolling of the ship were more than Hana could bear. Shuddering in the face of the wind, she leaned over the railing and became violently and wretchedly ill.

10
(John Okada, 1923—1971)
约翰·冈田

作者简介

约翰·冈田（John Okada，1923—1971），出生于西雅图，并在那里完成了自己的中学学业后，进入一所专科学校。太平洋战争爆发之后，冈田一家同其他日裔家庭一起被强制迁移，重新安置。在拘留营中，冈田志愿参军，从事日语语言翻译工作。1946年，冈田从军队退役，在华盛顿大学完成了自己的本科学业并于1949年在哥伦比亚大学获得了硕士学位。毕业之后的冈田为了谋生辗转于西雅图和底特律，但无论生活多么艰难，他都没有放弃写作。1956年，冈田的《不－不仔》（*No-No Boy*）完成并于次年出版，这是他的第一本也是唯一一本出版的小说。这部小说出版后并不受欢迎，赵健秀曾说这本小说"是一本出版之后立马被遗忘的作品，证据就是，小说出版后15年，第一版的1 500本书仍然没有卖完"。原因主要在于作者及其作品均生不逢时，出现在一个错误的年代。这个时期的日裔没人愿意回忆拘留营中的痛苦经历，而此时的美国媒体正试图将华裔和日裔美国人塑造成"模范少数族裔"，主流学界也早已忘记了日裔这一边缘群体所遭受的创伤。1971年赵健秀、劳森·稻田等人从旧书堆里将它重新发掘出来，并将这本小说的一个部分选入《哎咿！美国亚裔作家选集》（*Aiiieeeee! An Anthology of Asian American Writers*）中，引起了读者和学术界的极大关注，此后这本小说成为畅销书，并且成为大学里研读美国亚裔文学的重要文本。《不－不仔》是冈田唯一的作品，但是这部小说却足以确保他成为美国亚裔最杰出的小说家之一。

小说《不－不仔》讲述了美国日裔对自己身份的看法，以及他们在第二次世界大战期间被拘禁的经历对日裔群体的分化。主人公一郎（Ichiro Yamada）是一个美国日裔二世，第二次世界大战中被拘押在拘留营中。他因为在美国政府甄别日裔忠诚与否问卷中的两个重要问题说"不"，被判处两年监禁。出狱后一郎回到西雅图，他被日裔退伍军人歧视，也要与母亲斗争，因为她失去了理智，坚持认为日本没有输掉战争。冈田在小说中探讨了日本人的感受：一些一世仍然梦想着回到日本；二世则对自己的身份感到矛盾。两代人中有些人对他们在战争期间被拘留的经历，以及他们所遭受的巨大经济和社会损失感到极为痛苦。节选部分为本书第一章的开头部分，叙述了一郎出狱后在回家路上的遭遇。

作品选读

No-No Boy

1
(Excerpt)

TWO WEEKS AFTER HIS TWENTY-FIFTH BIRTHDAY, ICHIRO got off a bus at Second and Main in Seattle. He had been gone four years, two in camp and two in prison.

Walking down the street that autumn morning with a small, black suitcase, he felt like an intruder in a world to which he had no claim. It was just enough that he should feel this way, for, of his own free will, he had stood before the judge and said that he would not go in the army. At the time there was no other choice for him. That was when he was twenty-three, a man of twenty-three. Now, two years older, he was even more of a man.

Christ, he thought to himself, just a goddamn kid is all I was. Didn't know enough to wipe my own nose. What the hell have I done? What am I doing back here? Best thing I can do would be to kill some son of a bitch and head back to prison.

He walked toward the railroad depot where the tower with the clocks on all four sides was. It was a dirty looking tower of ancient brick. It was a dirty city. Dirtier, certainly, than it had a right to be after only four years.

Waiting for the light to change to green, he looked around at the people standing at the bus stop. A couple of men in suits, half a dozen women who failed to arouse him even after prolonged good behavior, and a young Japanese with a lunch bucket. Ichiro studied him, searching in his mind for the name that went with the round, pimply face and the short-cropped hair. The pimples were gone and the face had hardened, but the hair was still cropped. The fellow wore green, army-fatigue trousers and an Eisenhower jacket—Eto Minato. The name came to him at the same time as did the horrible significance of the army clothes. In panic, he started to step off the curb. It was too late. He had been seen.

"Itchy!" That was his nickname.

Trying to escape, Ichiro urged his legs frenziedly across the street.

"Hey, Itchy!" The caller's footsteps ran toward him.

An arm was placed across his back. Ichiro stopped and faced the other Japanese. He tried to smile, but could not. There was no way out now.

"I'm Eto. Remember?" Eto smiled and extended his palm. Reluctantly, Ichiro lifted his own hand and let the other shake it.

The round face with the round eyes peered at him through silver-rimmed spectacles. "What the hell! It's been a long time, but not that long. How've you been? What's doing?"

"Well... that is, I'm..."

"Last time must have been before Pearl Harbor. ..., it's been quite a while, hasn't it? Three, no, closer to four years, I guess. Lotsa Japs coming back to the Coast. Lotsa Japs in Seattle. You'll see 'em around. Japs are funny that way. Gotta have their rice and sake and other Japs. Stupid, I say. The smart ones went to Chicago and New York and lotsa places back east, but there's still plenty coming back out this way." Eto drew cigarettes from his breast pocket and held out the package. "No? Well, I'll have one. Got the habit in the army. Just got out a short while back. Rough time, but I made it. Didn't get out in time to make the quarter, but I'm planning to go to school. How long you been around?"

Ichiro touched his toe to the suitcase. "Just got in. Haven't been home yet."

"When'd you get discharged?"

A car grinding its gears started down the street. He wished he were in it. "I... that is... I never was in."

Eto slapped him good-naturedly on the arm. "No need to look so sour. So you weren't in. So what? Been in camp all this time?"

"No." He made an effort to be free of Eto with his questions. He felt as if he were in a small room whose walls were slowly closing in on him. "It's been a long time, I know, but I'm really anxious to see the folks."

"What the hell. Let's have a drink. On me. I don't give a damn if I'm late to work. As for your folks, you'll see them soon enough. You drink, don't you?"

"Yeah, but not now."

"Ahh." Eto was disappointed. He shifted his lunch box from under one arm to the other.

"I've really got to be going."

The round face wasn't smiling any more. It was thoughtful. The eyes confronted Ichiro with indecision which changed slowly to enlightenment and then to suspicion. He remembered. He knew.

The friendliness was gone as he said: "No-no boy, huh?"

Ichiro wanted to say yes. He wanted to return the look of despising hatred and say simply yes, but it was too much to say. The walls had closed in and were crushing all the unspoken words back down into his stomach. He shook his head once, not wanting to evade the eyes but finding it impossible to meet them. Out of his big weakness the little ones were branching, and the eyes he didn't have the courage to face were ever present. If it would have helped to gouge out his own eyes, he would have done so long ago. The hate-churned eyes with the stamp of unrelenting condemnation were his cross and he had driven the nails with his own hands.

"Rotten bastard. Shit on you." Eto coughed up a mouthful of sputum and rolled his words around it: "Rotten, no-good bastard."

Surprisingly, Ichiro felt relieved. Eto's anger seemed to serve as a release to his own naked tensions. As he stooped to lift the suitcase a wet wad splattered over his hand and dripped onto the black leather. The legs of his accuser were in front of him. ... in a pair of green fatigues, U. S. Army style. They were the legs of the jury that had passed sentence upon him. Beseech me, they seemed to say, throw your arms about me and bury your head between my knees and seek pardon for your great sin.

"I'll piss on you next time," said Eto vehemently.

He turned as he lifted the suitcase off the ground and hurried away from the legs and the eyes from which no escape was possible.

11

(Milton Murayama, 1923—2016)
弥尔顿·村山

作者简介

弥尔顿·村山（Milton Murayama, 1923—2016），出生在夏威夷毛伊岛（Maui）。父母是日本移民，父亲以捕鱼为生。村山小学的时候，父亲的捕鱼生意失败，入不敷出，因此一家人搬到了一个甘蔗种植园小镇，成为小镇上几百个甘蔗种植园工人家庭中的一个。小镇隶属于制糖公司，所有家庭的生活，包括住房、饮食等都依赖于制糖公司，因此各个家庭中的成年人基本都在糖厂或者甘蔗种植园里工作，忍受恶劣的环境和五大制糖公司资本家的剥削。1941年，村山进入夏威夷大学学习，但是不久珍珠港遭到日军突袭，太平洋战争爆发。村山报名参军，经过军事情报语言学校的培训，作为美军的一名翻译到中国和缅甸服役。第二次世界大战结束后，村山退役回到夏威夷大学完成自己的学业，并享受退役老兵福利，在哥伦比亚大学获得了汉语和日语硕士学位。随后，村山辗转到旧金山，成为一名海关关员。村山在哥伦比亚大学读书的时候就开始写作，但是他的第一部小说《我要的只是我的身体》（*All I Asking for Is My Body*, 1975）却屡次被拒绝。后来村山自费出版，一炮而红，极受读者以及评论家的欢迎，该书获得1980年哥伦布之前基金会颁发的美国图书奖以及1991年夏威夷文学奖。之后，村山又创作了两部戏剧《阿尔提雅》（*Althea*）和《义经》（*Yoshitsune*, 1977），以及三部小说《岩石上的五年》（*Five Years on a Rock*, 1994）、《种植园小伙子》（*Plantation Boy*, 1998）以及《死在异乡》（*Dying in a Strange Land*, 2008）。

村山最著名的小说《我要的只是我的身体》描述了第二次世界大战期间居住在夏威夷的一个贫穷美国日裔家庭的困境。小说分为三个部分，讲述了清代

（Kiyo）在夏威夷甘蔗种植园的成长故事。在第一部分中，清代与一个年龄稍长的男孩成为朋友，男孩的母亲是种植园的妓女；清代对父母反对他们的友谊感到困惑。在第二部分中，清代探索了他周围人的各种精神信仰体系。在第三部分，也是最长的部分中，清代的大哥俊雄（Toshio）与父母发生了冲突，父母希望他履行"孝道"来偿还家庭债务，但是俊雄声称，这笔钱是被他的祖父偷走的。俊雄以及清代都学了拳击，俊雄甚至可以成为职业拳手。然而，他为了帮助父母维持生计而放弃了拳击事业。清代最终加入了军队，并在一场兵营赌博比赛中赢了足够的钱，还清了家庭债务。

节选部分为小说的第一部分，清代一家因为父亲的捕鱼事业破产，不得不搬到种植园小镇生活。

作品选读

All I Asking for Is My Body

1

On August 1, 1936, another girl was born and father must've been a little disappointed. He named her *Tsuneko* (Common child). By the end of the month he decided to quit fishing and move the family back to Kahana where he'd first arrived in 1910. Tosh was to quit high school and work in the cane fields to help support the family. It was what every number one son was expected to do. Father had done it for twelve years, turning over his entire pay to grandfather every month. Even after mother was sent for in 1915 and even after Tosh was born in 1919, father gave grandfather all of his pay. It was a model story of filial piety, which mother told over and over. Great grandfather died while grandfather was in business college, and grandfather quit school and returned to the family farm in Wakayama, Japan. He was number one son and he inherited the farm, but he wasn't any good at farming and after a couple of years, he sold the farm. He married grandmother who was a couple of years older for her dowry, and he opened a clothing store in Osaka with the dowry and money from the farm. The store kept failing and he kept borrowing money from relatives and friends till he finally went broke seven years later. By then he had a huge debt and three young sons, father being number one. But he refused to declare bankruptcy, and promised every creditor he'd pay back every cent. He looked up *Obaban*, his older sister who'd been kicked out of the family, and wrote to her in Kahana. He left his children with relatives in Japan and came to Kahana in 1902 with grandmother. Three more children were born, and father and his two brothers were sent for, and sent to work in the cane fields. When grandfather finally saved enough money to return to Japan in 1922, mother begged him to leave father and her some money. She was carrying another child, and they had nothing to live on for the next month. Grandfather wept and he begged mother not to ask. He needed every penny he'd saved. He had all the debts he had to pay back in Japan, he had a family of two girls and one boy he was taking back with him. There were the boat fare, winter clothing and a hundred unforeseen expenses after which he had to have enough to open a clothing store in Tokyo. Not only that, he asked father to pay the bill for his farewell party, which came to $300; he asked father to look after his two younger brothers. He cried, "I'll repay you, I'll send for you as soon as I'm successful! I can't ask for more filial children!" "That's why," mother would say to us, "our minds are at peace even if he should die tomorrow. We've done our filial duty to him."

Moving to Kahana was a shock. The place had no indoor toilets, no private baths. It's what I hated most when I visited *Obaban* in the summer. I went with Mr. Hida of Hida Store in Pepelau, who drove there every Wednesday to deliver the orders he'd taken the week before. If I missed him, it meant I'd be stuck for a whole week. Now I was going to be stuck forever! Where I'd been only three blocks from the ocean in Pepelau, Kahana was two miles from the ocean up a pretty steep hill. In Pepelau the cane fields started beyond the plantation camps of Mill Camp, Ohia Camp, and Hau Camp, a good two miles from the center of town; in Kahana the cane fields surrounded you and they began right beyond your yard. It was like my childhood was chopped off clean.

In Pepelau we called the guys *bobora* (country bumpkins) who were too Japanese. In Kahana everybody was a *bobora*. Their heads looked bigger with their shorter haircuts. Most of the Japanese in Kahana had come there in the 1890's and 1900's from farming villages in Japan, and they were cut off from the world ever since. There were many different races in Pepelau, but Kahana had about one hundred Japanese families, about two hundred Filipino men, about seven Portuguese and Spanish families, and only two *haoles*. Mr. Boyle was the principal of the Kahana Grade School, and Mr. Nelson was the overseer of Kahana. There'd been many Chinese workers before, but they left and opened stores in Pepelau and the other towns as soon as their contracts expired.

It was a company town with identical company houses and outhouses, and it was set up like a pyramid. At the tip was Mr. Nelson, then the Portuguese, Spanish, and nisei *lunas* in their nicer-looking homes, then the identical wooden frame houses of Japanese Camp, then the more run-down Filipino Camp. There were a plantation store, a plantation mess hall for the Filipino bachelors, a plantation community bathhouse, and a plantation social hall. The *lunas* or strawbosses had their own baths and indoor toilets. There were a Catholic Church, the Japanese language school which became the Methodist Church on Sundays, a Buddhist hall, and a plantation dispensary which was open from 11 to 12 noon every working day.

The macadamized or "government" road ended in front of Mr. Nelson's big yard, and all the roads in camp were "plantation" roads, and the dirt was so red it stained your clothes and feet. The guys in Pepelau used to joke about how they could spot a guy from Kahana by his red feet. The place was so country they used newspaper for toilet paper, and each outhouse building was partitioned into four toilets. The rough one-by-sixteen planks used for the partitions did not go up to the rafters, and you could hear all the farts and everything going on in the other toilets. A three-foot-deep concrete ditch ran underneath all the toilets, and you sat back to back against a common partition with one of the other toilets. You were so close in fact you could touch the other guy's ass if you lifted the big square toilet seat. There were half a dozen rows of outhouses and the ditches under them were flushed downhill to a big concrete irrigation ditch which ran around the lower boundary of the camp, and sooner or later shit, newspaper and all ended up in the furrows of the fields below. The plantation had built pigpens along the four-foot-wide *kukai* ditch, and rented them to the workers. Every family kept pigs.

The house we moved into, No.173, was the last house on "Pig Pen Avenue" and next to the pigpens and ditch, and when the wind stopped blowing or when the warm Kona wind blew from the south, our house smelled like both an outhouse and a pigpen. Worse yet, the family debt was now $6,000, and the average plantation pay for forty-eight hours a week was $25 a month for adults. There was no sick pay, no holiday pay though you got off Christmas, New Year's, and one day during the County Fair in October.

I felt sorry for Tosh the first few months. He'd come home from the fields and collapse on the wooden floor in the parlor. A couple of times he skipped supper and bath, and slept right through in his denim work clothes covered with dust and stained with red sweat. The work clothes got so red and dirty, mother had to boil them for several hours on Saturdays. She'd done the same thing back in 1915 when she arrived from Japan.

12

(Wakako Yamauchi, 1924—2018)
山内若子

作者简介

山内若子（Wakako Yamauchi, 1924—2018，也译作山内和歌子）是美国日裔重要的戏剧家之一。她出生于加州韦斯特莫兰（Westmorland），父母都是加州国王谷（Imperial Valley）的一世日裔移民。第二次世界大战期间，17岁的山内同家人一起被关押在亚利桑那州波斯顿（Poston, Arizona）拘留营中。其间她结识了山本久枝并与其成为挚友。在波斯顿生活了一年半后，山内又在营地外定居，先是在犹他州，然后在芝加哥，在那里她开始对戏剧产生兴趣。第二次世界大战后山内回到西海岸定居，在此期间她创作了一部短篇小说《灵魂将要跳舞》（*And the Soul Shall Dance*）。这部小说后来被赵健秀等人选入《哎咿！美国亚裔作家选集》，并被山内改编成戏剧且获得极大成功，于1974年在洛杉矶东西方戏剧协会首次演出，并于1977年获得洛杉矶戏剧评论家奖最佳新剧奖，后来又被制作成公共电视节目。她的主要剧作还有《音乐课》（*The Music Lessons*）。1994年，她的作品集《我母亲教给我的歌：短篇小说、戏剧和回忆录》（*Songs My Mother Taught Me: Stories, Plays and Memoir*）出版，集中包含了她所有的作品。2018年，山内若子在加州去世，享年93岁。

山内作品的主题主要是美国日裔农场生活以及他们的拘留营经历。她的戏剧《音乐课》叙述了千津子（Chizuko）一家在美国西部沙漠农场中艰难谋生的故事。丈夫过世后，千津子与两个儿子、一个女儿依靠租赁的土地为生。丈夫留下的债务以及农场收入的不稳定使她不得不精打细算，将收入开支局限在家庭必需品上。兼有音乐家和流动工人双重身份的川口熏（Kaoru）以食宿为条件加入这个家庭，在被迫卷入与千津子和她未成年的女儿亚纪（Aki）之间的三角恋爱后，他被压制的情欲、愤怒与失望完全释放出来。下文节选部分为本剧的第一幕第二场，中村（Nakamura）向熏诉说日裔农场生活的艰辛。

作品选读

The Music Lessons

ACT I
Scene ii

October afternoon

ON RISE: *In Kaoru's shed. KAORU has just returned from town. He's dressed in his good clothes. It's his day off, and on the bed is a paper bag containing a small book of poems, magazines, some candy, and a pretty chiffon scarf. Kaoru's door is closed.*

NAKAMURA enters from stage left. He carries a small bottle of wine in his back pocket.

NAKAMURA: Chizuko-san… *[He opens the kitchen door and peers in.]* Chizuko-San!

KAORU *[opening his shed door]*: Hello!

NAKAMURA: Oh! Chizuko told me she hired you.

KAORU: Come in. Come in.

Continuing [NAKAMURA enters the shed.]

KAORU *[continuing]*: Been almost a month now. Been meaning to thank you. Today's my day off.

[NAKAMURA looks for a place to sit and picks up the paper bag.]

NAKAMURA: Been to town already, eh? Been shopping.

KAORU: Just some things for the kids. They don't get much of anything.

NAKAMURA: You're a good man, Kawa. *[He Looks in the bag.]*

KAORU: No-no. Nothing much.

NAKAMURA *[bringing out the book]*: What's this?

KAORU: For the girl. She likes to read.

    [NAKAMURA pulls out the scarf (which should show the kind of woman KAORU loves) and looks at KAORU qustioningly.]

KAORU *[continuing]*: Oh, that. Reminded me of someone I once knew. I'm thinking of sending it to her.

NAKAMURA: Oh, yeah? *[He drinks from his bottle.]*

KAORU: Maybe it's foolish.

NAKAMURA: No-no. *[He offers KAORU a sip.]* Where's Chizuko-san?

KAORU *[refusing the drink]*: I don't know. I just got back from town.

    [NAKAMURA looks around and lowers his voice.]

NAKAMURA: That woman never lets up. Works like a man. Maybe better, eh?

KAORU: Maybe.

NAKAMURA: Says she found a good man, Kawa. Thanked me for sending you down. *[He laughs raucously]* Yeah. Thinks we're old friends.

KAORU: I'm working hard. I'm going to try to get her a good harvest so I can make some money too.

NAKAMURA *[laughing hard]*: You think all you got to do to make money is to work hard? If that's the way, I'd be a millionaire now.

KAORU: You don't have to be a millionaire to have a farm. I want to save some money and start my own place.

    [NAKAMURA scoffs.]

KAORU *[continuing]*: Sure. I'll work here a while and get the feel of it; save my money and...

NAKAMURA: "Save!" Horseshit! Only way to do is borrow money.

KAORU: Who's going to lend me money? I got nothing. No collateral.

NAKAMURA: Well, first you get some names together. Good names. You can use mine. Sponsors, you know? Then you go to a produce company—in Los Angeles. That's where they all are. Put on a good suit, talk big... how you going to make big money for them. Get in debt. Then you pay back after the harvest. *[The futility of it occurs to him.]* Then you borrow again next year. Then you pay back. If you can. Same thing again next year. You never get the farm. The farm gets you. *[He drinks.]*

KAORU: You never get the farm?

NAKAMURA: 'S true. Orientals can't own land here. It's the law.

KAORU: The law? Then how is it that (you)...

NAKAMURA: Well, I lease. If you have a son old enough, you can buy land under his name. He's 'Merican citizen, you see? That's if you have enough money.

KAORU: I'll apply for citizenship then.

NAKAMURA: There's a law against that too. Orientals can't be citizens.

KAORU: We can't?

NAKAMURA: That's the law. Didn't you know?

> *[NAKAMURA again offers KAORU a drink. This time he accepts and drains the bottle. NAKAMURA looks at the empty bottle.]*

NAKAMURA *[continuing]*: Hey, let's go to town.

KAORU: I just came from there.

NAKAMURA: Yeah, me too. Come on, we'll get some more wine. *[He lowers his voice.]* You know, Chizuko don't like drinking. Her old man used to *[ha-ha]* drink a little. Like me. He drowned in a canal, you know. Fell off a catwalk.

KAORU *[putting on his coat]*: Is that right?

NAKAMURA: Yeah, six... almost seven years ago.

KAORU: That long?

NAKAMURA: Yeah. She got lucky with tomatoes a couple of years ago and paid back all her old man's debts. People never expected to see their money again, but she did it. She paid them back. Now she never borrows—lives close to the belly—stingy, tight. That's the way she stays ahead. Not much ahead, but...

> *[They exit talking.]*

KAORU: That so?

NAKAMURA: What's she planting this year?

KAORU: Squash, tomatoes...

NAKAMURA: Tomatoes again?

13

(Jeanne Wakatsuki Houston, 1934—)
珍妮·若月·休斯敦

作者简介

  珍妮·若月·休斯敦（Jeanne Wakatsuki Houston, 1934—）是著名的日裔自传作家，出生于加利福尼亚州英格伍德（Inglewood, California）一个依靠捕鱼为生的美国日裔家庭。太平洋战争爆发之后，七岁的她与父母一起被强制迁徙并关押在曼扎那拘留营中，这是一段她不愿回想但又难以忘怀的记忆。珍妮在小学和高中成绩优异。她在圣何塞州立大学（San Jose State College）学习社会学和新闻学，在那里她遇到了未来的丈夫詹姆斯·D. 休斯敦（James D. Houston），并于1957年结婚。后来，在丈夫的鼓励与协助下，她将自己的个人经历写成了《永别了，曼扎那》（*Farewell to Manzanar*, 1973）一书。

  《永别了，曼扎那》描述了第二次世界大战期间，美国日裔在拘留营中的生活经历。虽然这本书主要是自传性的，重点关注若月一家，但作者从更大的历史角度对拘留经历进行了考察。与其他有关日裔美国人战时被监禁的类似报道一样，《永别了，曼扎那》不仅谴责了对日裔的拘禁，还探讨种族主义在美国政府执行行政命令中的作用。休斯敦夫妇对比了若月夫妇在被拘留和战争之前、期间和之后的不同生活方式，详细描述了珍妮和她的家人在父亲被捕并随后被关押之前不太完美但幸福的生活。她记录了自己与种族和文化身份的斗争，以及她融入主流文化的努力，希望自己能够被种族分裂的社会接受。在传记的结尾，珍妮与丈夫和三个孩子一起回到集中营，从而在生理和心理上终结了她自认为是可耻的拘留营生活经历。

  节选部分是自传的第12节，叙述了作者初到曼扎那拘留营的所见与所感。

作品选读

Farewell to Manzanar

Manzanar, U. S. A.
(Excerpt)

In Spanish, Manzanar means "apple orchard." Great stretches of Owens Valley were once green with orchards and alfalfa fields. It has been a desert ever since its water started flowing south into Los Angeles, sometime during the twenties. But a few rows of untended pear and apple trees were still growing there when the camp opened, where a shallow water table had kept them alive. In the spring of 1943 we moved to Block 28, right up next to one of the old pear orchards. That's where we stayed until the end of the war, and those trees stand in my memory for the turning of our life in camp, from the outrageous to the tolerable.

Papa pruned and cared for the nearest trees. Late that summer we picked the fruit green and stored it in a root cellar he had dug under our new barracks. At night the wind through the leaves would sound like the surf had sounded in Ocean Park, and while drifting off to sleep I could almost imagine we were still living by the beach.

Mama had set up this move. Block 28 was also close to the camp hospital. For the most part, people lived there who had to have easy access to it. Mama's connection was her job as dietician. A whole half of one barracks had fallen empty when another family relocated. Mama hustled us in there almost before they'd snapped their suitcases shut.

For all the pain it caused, the loyalty oath finally did speed up the relocation program. One result was a gradual easing of the congestion in the barracks. A shrewd house-hunter like Mama could set things up fairly comfortably—by Manzanar standards—if she kept her eyes open. But you had to move fast. As soon as the word got around that so-and-so had been cleared to leave, there would be a kind of tribal restlessness, a nervous rise in the level of neighborhood gossip as wives jockeyed for position to see who would get the empty cubicles.

In Block 28 we doubled our living space—four rooms for the twelve of us. Ray and Woody walled them with sheetrock. We had ceilings this time, and linoleum floors of solid maroon. You had three colors to choose from—maroon, black, and forest green—and there was plenty of it around by this time. Some families would vie with one another for the most elegant floor designs, obtaining a roll of each color from the supply shed, cutting it into diamonds, squares, or triangles, shining it with heating oil, then leaving their doors open so that passers-by could admire the handiwork.

Papa brought his still with him when we moved. He set it up behind the door, where he continued to brew his own sake and brandy. He wasn't drinking as much now, though. He spent a lot of time outdoors. Like many of the older Issei men, he didn't take a regular job in camp. He puttered. He had been working hard for thirty years and, bad as it was for him in some ways, camp did allow him time to dabble with hobbies he would never have found time for otherwise.

Once the first year's turmoil cooled down, the authorities started letting us outside the wire for recreation. Papa used to hike along the creeks that channeled down from the base of the Sierras. He brought back chunks of driftwood, and he would pass long hours sitting on the steps carving myrtle limbs into benches, table legs, and lamps, filling our rooms with bits of gnarled, polished furniture.

He hauled stones in off the desert and built a small rock garden outside our doorway, with succulents and a patch of moss. Near it he laid flat steppingstones leading to the stairs.

He also painted watercolors. Until this time I had not known he could paint. He loved to sketch the mountains. If anything made that country habitable it was the mountains themselves, purple when the sun dropped and so sharply etched in the morning light the granite dazzled almost more than the bright snow lacing it. The nearest peaks rose ten thousand feet higher than the valley floor, with Whitney, the highest, just off to the south. They were important for all of us, but especially for the Issei. Whitney reminded Papa of Fujiyama, that is, it gave him the same kind of spiritual sustenance. The tremendous beauty of those peaks was inspirational, as so many natural forms are to the Japanese (the rocks outside our doorway could be those mountains in miniature). They also represented those forces in nature, those powerful and inevitable forces that cannot be resisted, reminding a man that sometimes he must simply endure that which cannot be changed.

Subdued, resigned, Papa's life—all our lives—took on a pattern that would hold for the duration of the war. Public shows of resentment pretty much spent themselves over the loyalty oath crises. *Shikata ga nai* again became the motto, but under altered circumstances. What had to be endured was the climate, the confinement, the steady crumbling away of family life. But the camp itself had been made livable. The government provided for our physical needs. My parents and older brothers and sisters, like most of the internees, accepted their lot and did what they could to make the best of a bad situation. "We're here," Woody would say. "We're here, and there's no use moaning about it forever."

Gardens had sprung up everywhere, in the firebreaks, between the rows of barracks—rock gardens, vegetable gardens, cactus and flower gardens. People who lived in Owens Valley during the war still remember the flowers and lush greenery they could see from the highway as they drove past the main gate. The soil around Manzanar is alluvial and very rich. With water siphoned off from the Los Angeles-bound aqueduct, a large farm was under cultivation just outside the camp, providing the mess halls with lettuce, corn, tomatoes, eggplant, string beans, horseradish, and cucumbers. Near Block 28 some of the men who had been professional gardeners built a small park, with mossy nooks, ponds, waterfalls and curved wooden bridges. Sometimes in the evenings we could walk down the raked gravel paths. You could face away from the barracks, look past a tiny rapids toward the darkening mountains, and for a while not be a prisoner at all. You could hang suspended in some odd, almost lovely land you could not escape from yet almost didn't want to leave.

As the months at Manzanar turned to years, it became a world unto itself, with its own logic and familiar ways. In time, staying there seemed far simpler than moving once again to another, unknown place. It was as if the war were forgotten, our reason for being there forgotten. The present, the little bit of busywork you had right in front of you, became the most urgent thing. In such a narrowed world, in order to survive, you learn to contain your rage and your despair, and you try to re-create, as well as you can, your normality, some sense of things continuing. The fact that America had accused us, or excluded us, or imprisoned us, or whatever it might be called, did not change the kind of world we wanted. Most of us were born in this country; we had no other models. Those parks and gardens lent it an oriental character, but in most ways it was a totally equipped American small town, complete with schools, churches, Boy Scouts, beauty parlors, neighborhood gossip, fire and police departments, glee clubs, softball leagues, Abbott and Costello movies, tennis courts, and traveling shows. (I still remember an Indian who turned up one Saturday billing himself as a Sioux chief, wearing bear claws and head feathers. In the firebreak he sang songs and danced his tribal dances while hundreds of us watched.)

In our family, while Papa puttered, Mama made her daily rounds to the mess halls, helping young mothers with their feeding, planning diets for the various ailments people suffered from. She wore a bright yellow, longbilled sun hat she had made herself and always kept stiffly starched. Afternoons I would see her coming from blocks away, heading home, her tiny figure warped by heat waves and that bonnet a yellow flower wavering in the glare.

14

(Lawson Fusao Inada, 1938—)
劳森·稻田

作者简介

劳森·稻田（Lawson Fusao Inada, 1938— ）是一名诗人、学者，2006年被评为俄勒冈州的桂冠诗人。稻田于1938年出生于加州弗雷斯诺（Fresno），他很小的时候同父母一起被关入集中营中。第二次世界大战后，稻田回到弗雷斯诺，在那里生活了15年。他于1959年毕业于位于弗雷斯诺的加州州立大学；从1960到1962年，他在艾奥瓦大学获得奖学金进行研究生学习，但直到1966年他才完成研究生教育，在俄勒冈大学获得艺术硕士学位。稻田被很多人尊崇为"美国亚裔诗歌之父"，目前已经出版了三部诗集：《战前》（*Before the War*, 1971）、《拘留营传奇》（*Legends from Camp*, 1992）以及《划线》（*Drawing the Line: Poems*, 1997）。作为一名学者，稻田对美国亚裔文学的发展与研究做出了杰出的贡献，他与赵健秀等人一起编写了《哎咿！美国亚裔作家选集》和《大哎咿！美国华裔和日裔作家选集》（*The Big Aiiieeeee! An Anthology of Chinese-American and Japanese-American Literature*, 1991）。

稻田诗歌创作中审视和阐释的焦点是第二次世界大战期间美国日裔被强制迁徙、非法拘禁这些令人感到激愤的事件。《战前》诗集中许多诗歌描绘了与拘留营有关的事物，以及后来对拘留营的反思。其他诗歌则涉及爱情关系和对孩子出生的渴望等主题。《拘留营传奇》由"营地"、"弗雷斯诺"、"爵士乐"、"俄勒冈"和"表演"等五个部分组成，描绘了家庭、艺术和爵士乐主题，许多作品涉及诗人从一个地方到另一个地方的运动，以及他工作中受到的艺术影响。稻田将地理、家族史、战争政治和个人生活都融合在一起，对美国制度化的种族主义和对美国日裔的非法拘留进行了有力的批判。

节选部分为《拘留营传奇》中的《序曲》，主要叙述了美国日裔在太平洋战争爆发后被美国政府非法拘禁、强制迁徙的人数、地点等。

作品选读

Legends from Camp

Prologue

1 It began as truth, as fact.
2 That is, at least the numbers, the statistics,
3 are there for verification:

4 10 camps, 7 states,
5 120,113 residents.

6 Still, figures can lie: people are born, die.
7 And as for the names of the places themselves,
8 these, too, were subject to change:

9 Denson or Jerome, Arkansas;
10 Gila or Canal, Arizona;
11 Tule Lake or Newell, California;
12 Amache or Granada, Colorado.

13 As was the War Relocation Authority
14 with its mention of "camps" or "centers" for:

15 Assembly,
16 Concentration,
17 Detention,

18　Evacuation,
19　Internment,
20　Relocation, —
21　among others.

[[22]] "Among others"—that's important also. Therefore, let's not forget contractors, carpenters, plumbers, electricians and architects, sewage engineers, and all the untold thousands who provided the materials, decisions, energy, and transportation to make the camps a success, including, of course, the administrators, clerks, and families who not only swelled the population but were there to make and keep things shipshape according to D. C. directives and people deploying coffee in the various offices of the WRA, overlooking, overseeing rivers, cityscapes, bays, whereas in actual camp the troops—excluding, of course, our aunts and uncles and sisters and brothers and fathers and mothers serving stateside, in the South Pacific, the European theater—pretty much had things in order; finally, there were the grandparents, who since the turn of the century, simply assumed they were living in America "among others."

23　The situation, obviously, was rather confusing.
24　It obviously confused simple people
25　who had simply assumed they were friends, neighbors,
26　colleagues, partners, patients, customers, students,
27　teachers, of, not so much "aliens" or "non-aliens,"
28　but likewise simple, unassuming people
29　who paid taxes as fellow citizens and populated
30　pews and desks and fields and places
31　of ordinary American society and commerce.

32　Rumors flew. Landed. What's what? Who's next?

33　And then, "just like that," it happened.
34　And then, "just like that," it was over.
35　Sun, moon, stars—they came, and went.

36　And then, and then, things happened,
37　and as they ended they kept happening,

38 and as they happened they ended
39 and began again, happening, happening,

40 until the event, the experience, the history,
41 slowly began to lose its memory,
42 gradually drifting into a kind of fiction—

43 a "true story based on fact,"
44 but nevertheless with "all the elements of fiction"—
45 and then, and then, sun, moon, stars,
46 we come, we come, to where we are:
47 Legend.

15

(Lonny Kaneko, 1939—2017)
罗尼·金子

作者简介

罗尼·金子（Lonny Kaneko, 1939—2017）是美国日裔诗人和短篇小说作家，出生于华盛顿州西雅图。第二次世界大战爆发后，他只有三岁，和父母一起被强制迁徙重新安置，关在艾奥瓦州的米尼多卡（Minidoka）拘留营。金子于 1960 年开始创作诗歌。1963 年，他在华盛顿大学（University of Washington）获得了英语硕士学位。他的大部分零散诗歌都是在 20 世纪七八十年代发表。1986 年，他出版了自己唯一的诗集《自拘留营返乡》(*Coming Home from Camp*)。20 世纪 90 年代，他又创作了几首诗和几篇短篇小说，其中《酱油小子》("The Shoyu Kid")最为知名。金子获得过诸多奖项：1973 年，科达伦艺术节诗歌比赛冠军（the Coeur d'Alene Festival of Arts poetry contest）；1975 年，《亚美学刊》短篇小说比赛冠军；1981 年，他还获得了美国国家艺术基金会（National Endowment for the Arts）的奖学金。

金子的《酱油小子》是一个成长故事，讲述一个日裔少年在拘留营中遭到看守士兵性侵犯的故事。故事是由一个叫正雄（Masao）的少年以第一人称叙述者讲述的。正雄和朋友弘志（Hiroshi）、一郎（Ichiro）试图找出被他们称为"酱油小子"的小孩每天都有巧克力吃的秘密。最后，"酱油小子"向叙述者及其朋友们透露，巧克力棒是一个红头发士兵送给他的，作为他和士兵的"黑猩猩"（阴茎）玩耍的报酬。金子通过叙述这个拘留营里的背叛故事，突出了那些有权力的人（比如白人士兵）和那些没有权力的人（美国日裔，尤其是儿童）之间的对立。

作品选读

The Shoyu Kid
(Excerpt)

We were ready for him. The three of us were crouched in the vines, expecting the Kid to come stumbling into the garden. Itchy was to my right trying to tell me about what he'd seen earlier in the morning. Something about the sun rising from the wrong direction. I was too busy looking for the Kid to pay much attention. Jackson was in front of Itchy, ready to close off the Kid's escape in case he should see us before we could jump him. He came this way everyday. Usually when there was nothing else to do he would wander into the patch and sit down in the heat of the late morning sun and pull out a chocolate bar and eat it slowly so that by the time he finished his face and hands were streaked gooey brown. There was a dark lingering haze on the western horizon, and I wondered if it would rain.

"Here he comes."

"Shhh."

"Get your butt down. Shit, I think he heard us."

The Kid had stopped at the edge of the walk and was looking around. His dirty cotton bib coveralls billowed loosely over bare, unwashed feet. I couldn't see his eyes, but I knew they were watery. They always were. The Kid was always on the verge of crying. And he usually had his arms full of dog, his skinny weiner dog that Jackson nicknamed Kraut.

"Shut up."

The Kid stopped about six feet in front of Jackson, still too far away for Jackson to nab him. I heard him drawing the snot back into his nose. It was his trademark, that sniffing. He sounded like the old men who snuff tobacco. Itchy flattened his face in the dirt, and I did the same, holding my breath, trying not to inhale the dust that rose over the ground. It was already coating my tongue. The vines coiled around my right wrist and reached inside the back of my shirt.

We waited a long time. When I looked up, the Kid was gone.

"Hey, where'd he go?"

"I donno."

"That way. Around the building." Jackson was up and flying down the edge of the garden with Itchy and me not far behind. At the corner of the building, he pulled up, flattened himself against the wall and like a soldier in a war movie, peered around the corner. We pulled up behind him, puffing, and he turned and put a finger to his lips and inched an eye like a periscope around the corner. His body relaxed, and he turned back to us. "He's gone."

"Which way'd he go?"

"Maybe he turned up one of the rows."

So we ran half the length of the block, checking the walkways between the barracks to see if the Kid had turned up one of them. Nothing but a couple of girls the Kid's age trying to skip rope and Glen Miller music from the window of one of the barracks. We skirted three old women, who, like old women, stood in the shade of the barracks talking. It was already too hot for them to be out weeding the gardens. Jackson always greeted the women smoothly.

"Good morning, obasan," and they in return flashed smiles, and as if on cue made some comment in Japanese about Ichiro and Hiroshi and Masao growing up to be fine lads. Jackson hated to be called Hiroshi and would make a face or thumb his nose as soon as they turned their backs, but today he was too puzzled about the Kid's disappearing to remember his ritual.

"Hey, let's try over there." Itchy was pointing to the large garage and storage area that stood at right angles to the rows of barracks. We ran across the road to the garage—I guess that's what it was because Furuta, the cop, used to leave his car there. Beyond the garage was a road that was part of the system that connected all of the blocks of barracks and beyond that was the fence that surrounded our whole camp. When we first arrived, soldiers used to march around the fence. In the distance were hills that stretched as far as we could see. The past few days the hills had been covered with sheep so white that the hills had blended with the clouds. But this morning the sheep were gone, leaving us alone in the middle of a wide saucer of gray, overgrazed rangeland.

"C'mon. The Kid must be behind the building." Itchy pulled at my arm.

"But we aren't supposed to go over there."

"You're chicken. There aren't any more soldiers patrolling that fence."

"Geez, I know that."

"Well, I'm going to look." Itchy took off and pressed up against the side of the garage as Jackson had done before. Jackson followed, crouching like a cat stalking prey. And I went too.

Itchy was already peering around the corner like an Indian from behind a tree, when his body went stiff. He motioned us back, but he stayed fixed at the corner for another minute; then he took off past us running as hard as he could. Jackson and I turned and ran too. Itchy turned the corner of the garage, cut across the street, zagged past the second row of barracks and cut into the walkway in front of the third, almost hitting the old women and stumbling over one of the girls with the rope. We followed as fast as we could. I heard a shout and a dog barking behind us and urged my palomino to even greater speeds, following Itchy's dust. At the end of the third barrack we cut down the middle of the block and slipped into the side door of the laundry room where Jackson slowed so suddenly I almost galloped over him.

Mrs. Furuta had her little girl in a cast iron laundry tub, giving her a bath, and Jackson as he always did, stopped to take a look at the girl's naked body. Not obviously. He just strolled past Mrs. Furuta, said "Good morning, is Joyce having a bath?" just as if he couldn't tell what was happening in front of his eyes, and Mrs. Furuta said in Japanese "Go. Get out of here. You aren't supposed to play here," and we turned and ran on through and out the back door. At the door Jackson stopped and gave Mrs. Furuta's bent back the finger.

Jackson circled the laundry building, peered in through the window to get another look, then went into a cowboy pose, his thumbs hooked into his pockets.

Itchy, who had run straight through the building, was waiting for us. "Is anybody following us?"

"Nyaa."

"Hey, Itchy, what were we running for?"

'Nothing."

"Nothing?"

"C'mon, what happened?"

"Did you see Joyce?" Itchy was changing the subject. "Little girls are sure funny to look at, aren't they?"

"Itchy, you act like you ain't never seen a naked girl before."

"Well, have you? I mean really seen one, Jackson? Seen what kind of prick they have?"

"They don't have one."

"That's what I mean. Do you know what to do with it?"

"Everyone knows. You get this hard on, see, and…"

"Jackson, you got a hard on?" Itchy's face was tight.

"Yeah, don't you? You're supposed to."

"N-no."

"What are you, Itchy, some kind of queer or something. Don't you know you're supposed to have a hard on when you see a naked girl?" Jackson was getting wound up on his favorite subject. I sneaked a look at Jackson, and I think he was lying.

"Hey, Itchy, what'd you see?" I was still curious what we were running from. "Was the Kid back of the garage?"

"Kinda."

"What do you mean, kinda?"

"There was a soldier back there."

"A soldier? And the Kid?"

"He was there, too."

"Yeah?"

"And he had a chocolate bar."

"So that's where he gets them."

"Yeah."

"Maybe we can get some, too." Jackson was coming to life again. "Who was the soldier?"

"That red-headed one."

"What the hell was he doing way over here?" Jackson took great pains to sound like his older brother sometimes. "They don't patrol here any more. They're supposed to stay by the gate. Let's check it out tomorrow. Maybe he'll give us some too."

"Uh, no thanks."

"Why not, Itchy? Chicken?"

"Kinda."

"Whaddayou mean, Itchy? Shit, talk plain will you?" Jackson was leaning into Itchy.

"There's something strange about that guy. I mean that's the same red-headed soldier who used to stand there at the fence and point his gun at me like he was going to shoot."

I remembered that, too. So did Jackson. It was enough to make us nervous. "Well, how does the Kid do it? Maybe the guy's changed. Let's ask the Kid."

"Are you kidding? That snot-nosed brat. Makes me nervous to look at him, too."

I knew what Itchy meant. The Kid always had that heavy snot dripping from his nose. Like a perpetual cold. Except that the snot was the color of soy sauce. Jackson's older brother told him the reason the Kid had brown snot was because he used too much soy sauce, and it just dripped out of his nose. We all stopped using shoyu when we heard that.

The Kid used to follow us around all the time as if he were a pet. And Jackson would get him to bring food from the lunch line or steal pies. Then the Kid quit hanging around like he used to and he started showing up with the chocolate candy every now and then. His mother used to make him wear white shirts and polished shoes, but I guess the dust must have gotten to her, and she gave up. Later, I thought it was the chocolate that made the Kid's snot brown because it didn't used to be when he trailed after us.

"Ichirooo! Ichirooo!" It was Itchy's mother calling him for lunch so we decided to meet later at the clubhouse. Actually there was no house, just a place by the bridge over the irrigation ditch, on the far edge of the garden that we had marked with a couple of stolen signs. I was sure Itchy hadn't told us everything; so after he left, Jackson and I made a pact to be sure to get Itchy to spill what he had seen.

16

(Momoko Iko, 1940—)
伊川桃子

作者简介

伊川桃子（Momoko Iko, 1940— ）出生于华盛顿州瓦帕托（Wapato, Washington）的一个日本家庭。两岁的时候她就跟家人一起被关入怀俄明州的哈特山拘留营（Heart Mountain concentration camp, Wyoming）中。年幼的她自然不会对拘留营有太多太深刻的印象，但拘留营是她的写作中无法回避的一个题材。伊川在北伊利诺伊州接受大学教育，1961年在伊利诺伊大学厄巴纳－香槟分校（University of Illinois at Urbana-Champaign）获得英语学士学位。她还曾在墨西哥阿连德学院（Mexico's Instituto Allende）和艾奥瓦大学（University of Iowa）学习创意写作课程。1972年，她将自己一部未出版的小说改编为两幕剧《金表》（Gold Watch），这是日裔最早发表的剧作之一。她未出版的手稿包括《当我们年轻时》（When We Were Young, 1973）、《花与家庭之神》（Flowers and Household Gods, 1975）、《第二城市公寓》（Second City Flat, 1976）、《好莱坞之镜》（Hollywood Mirrors, 1978）、《精品生活与一次性偶像》（Boutique Living and Disposable Icons, 1987）。伊川曾获得过洛克菲勒基金会、泽勒巴赫基金会和国家艺术基金会的奖学金以及东西方演员协会颁发的奖项。

《金表》讲述了一个美国日裔社区从1941年秋天到1942年晚春这段时间内发生的故事。主人公村上真寿（Masu Murakami）是一个要强但贫穷的农民，与城里经营一家日本杂货店和干货商店的田中先生（Tanaka）是好朋友。剧中最初的冲突围绕着村上不愿意让他的二世儿子忠雄（Tadao）去买渴望已久的足球鞋展开。珍珠港事件后，父子冲突变得更加严重，忠雄和社区里的其他人无法忍受针对日裔言语和身体的攻击，主张他们应该回到日本，而村上坚决拒绝。此时针对日本社区的暴力事件不断增加，加上政府违背让农民能够收割本季庄稼的承诺，因此村上不再相信政府会保护日裔财产的承诺。于是他开始领导社区居民反对政府的强制迁移命令。村上在与破坏日裔财产的夜行者战斗中被杀之后，儿子忠雄成为了金表的主人。这部剧颂扬了日裔为家庭、尊严而斗争的勇气。

节选部分为第二幕的选段，社区居民开始讨论针对日裔的暴力事件和政府的强制迁徙令。

作品选读

Gold Watch

Act Two
(Excerpt)

Time: Late spring, 1942

At entrance to church basement where there is a table/lectern in front and American flag. Chairs are set up for meeting. Setsuko Tanaka and Reverend Sugano wait for Masu.

SETSUKO: They put sugar in Shimizu's tractor—why does he have to go around saying: *Yat-ta-do! Yat-ta-do!*

Masu enters.

REVEREND SUGANO: Stupid, plain stupid, talking out of turn.

SETSUKO: And they broke in Kagawa's tool shed.

TANAKA: *Chikisho!*

REVEREND SUGANO: Now, Tanaka-san, keep your head.

MASU: What did they say?

TANAKA: We have six days.

MASU: Six days... how? How are vegetables to be ripe, picked, crated, and sold in six days?

TANAKA: Other communities had two days...

MASU: Answer the question! Did you negotiate? I thought it was agreed; if we planted, we would harvest.

TANAKA: Masu, I tried. Some things can't be helped.

MASU: Don't say it, Tane!

TANAKA: It's been hard for all of us... you know that!

REVEREND SUGANO: It's not Tanaka-san's fault. The rules keep changing every day. No one is sure from day to day.

MASU: I heard that, General George Armstrong Custer! Military necessity! First it was evacuate, go inland. Then, no one can leave without army permission. We would be allowed to stay, work our farms, be protected from the scavengers. They're toying with our lives, Tane.

TANAKA: The reverend is right. We must go along.

REVEREND SUGANO: That's why we wanted to talk to you before the meeting. People listen to you.

MASU: (*ignoring Sugano*) Go along?

REVEREND SUGANO: Murakami-san, things are confused. Everything is terrible. These are bad times. His own son still wants to leave home, go back to Japan, join the Imperial Army. It is worse for you and the other farmers, but there must be someone to keep a level mind.

TANAKA: I'll store your equipment with my merchandise. The government has storage depots.

MASU: Store goods? Who will ever buy them? Mice? Listen to me, Tane... listen to one who is not sane, so level-minded. In insane times, listen to me.

REVEREND SUGANO: Murakami-san, this is not a year's crop.

MASU: I know that!

REVEREND SUGANO: The more mature the grain, the lower the head hangs.

MASU: (*under*) *Kusokue*

TANAKA: Masu, go along.

MASU: (*to Tanaka*) So you are listening to him again.

MASU: (*to Reverend Sugano*) Proverbs are the answers of dead men!

Masu leaves.

TANAKA: Masu, reconsider!

Lights fade and rise on church basement—before dusk—same day. People of community begin to enter the church meeting hall. The theater itself can be considered the hall, with the actors at strategic points in the audience. Crowd enters from different entrances in groups and scatters. Enter group A: M.1, M.2,

M.3, W.1 (wife of M.3) and W.2.

MAN 1: Did you hear about Kagawa?

MAN 2: Worse than the Shimizus?

MAN 1: He went into that bar after the sign went up, and they beat him up.

MAN 2: He and Shimizu were always pushy. The nail that sticks its head up, gets pounded down.

Man 4 enters to join group A.

MAN 4: That *yat-ta-do* fool. Shimizu deserved what he got!

MAN 1: Shame ... how can anyone say that?

MAN 4: He should have watched his tongue.

MAN 3: The seed store wouldn't refund our money.

MAN 2: I don't believe that. They have been good to me.

WOMAN 1: If Kagawa-san had a wife, everything would be different.

Group B: W.3, W.4 enter.

WOMAN 2: Well, what do you think? They say we'll have to leave.

WOMAN 3: No... no!

WOMAN 2: I hear in California...

WOMAN 3: (*cutting in*) Rumors... just rumors...

MAN 4: (*to woman* 2) I said so. Your husband should have sold early like me. It's your own fault.

Man 4 moves to another part of hall.

WOMAN 4: My children blame Japan. They say Japan makes trouble for us.

Group C: Mr. and Mrs. Shimizu enter. Mrs. Shimizu goes toward women, Mr. Shimizu toward men.

MRS. SHIMIZU: (*crying*) Burning down our shed, putting sugar in our tractor. Why are there such terrible men? What did we do?

WOMAN 2: Now, now, don't blame yourself... ... will punish them.

MRS. SHIMIZU: But what will we do?

Enters Kagawa, reassures Mrs. Shimizu and goes with her to Mr. Shimizu. Leaves her with Mr. Shimizu and Setsuko and goes to side of hall.

REVEREND SUGANO: (*at table*) Please, please, sit down ... please.

Some community members seat themselves, others stand, or lean against posts.

Members of this community and church. We face trying days ahead, and we must look to our inner resources to help guide us now. Let us have a silent prayer. (*ad libbing prayer*) Now, I have to tell you, we will have to leave here and go into camps.

A confusion of reactions. Hiroshi enters.

SHIMIZU: They're going to take us to the mountains and shoot us.

SETSUKO: Don't be silly.

Goes off to join group D: M.5, M.6 and W.5 (wife of M.6), M.7.

MAN 5: They say they built camps out where no one can see them.

MAN 6: That's what I heard.

WOMAN 4: (*to no one in particular*) They're going to put us in camps?

MAN 7: What are the Buddhists going to do?

WOMAN 5: Jiro Yamada went to Utah. I told you we should have gone inland when we had a chance.

MAN 6: Leave me alone.

Group remix: Setsuko, M.7, W.5, W.2, M.5.

SETSUKO: Don't cry.

WOMAN 5: They're going to shoot us!

SETSUKO: No, no, rumors! Irresponsible rumors!

MAN 5: They put some city people in buses with red flags and curtains pulled down so nobody could see inside. Tell me what that means!

SETSUKO: To protect us. So the *hakujins* can't see us and get mad.

WIFE 5: Oh, no! Right after Pearl Harbor, they take away my brother in Seattle. His wife ask and ask, but they don't tell her nothing.

REVEREND SUGANO: Please, please, as long as we cooperate, we have nothing to worry about. Let Tanaka-san explain to us the way we will get ready.

Sugano sits down.

TANAKA: (*going to table/lectern*) Yes, now, if we all stay calm, everything will be all right.

MAN 7: What are they doing at the temple?

MAN 1: It must be bad. Tanaka-san is not smiling.

TANAKA: The official name of the order is: Civilian Exclusion Order 9066.

KAGAWA: Get on with it!

Agreement by others.

TANAKA: What it says is that we must all register and report in at Portland Assembly Center six days from now. There we will learn exactly where we are to go.

17

(Janice Mirikitani, 1941—2021)
美里木古

作者简介

美里木古（Janice Mirikitani，1941—2021）是著名美国日裔三世诗人和活动家，她出生于加州的斯托克顿，父母经营农场，太平洋战争爆发后同父母一起被关入拘留营。20世纪60年代初，美里木古获得了加州大学洛杉矶分校的学士学位，并于1963年获得加州大学伯克利分校的教师资格证书。后来，她在旧金山州立大学（San Francisco State University）攻读创意写作研究生课程，并加入了美国亚裔政治联盟（Asian American Political Alliance），开始积极发声，抗议美国政府第二次世界大战期间针对日裔的暴行。她既关注社会问题，也热衷于各种政治议题。她的诗歌特别关注拘留营经历对日裔女性的影响，反对性别歧视，同时也谴责、控诉美国社会由来已久的种族歧视。迄今为止，美里木古已经出版了五部诗集：《在河中醒来》（*Awake in the River*, 1978）、《抛弃沉默》（*Shedding Silence*, 1987）、《危险的我们》（*We, the Dangerous*, 1995）、《爱是有用的》（*Love Works*, 2002）、《超越可能》（*Beyond the Possible*, 2013）。美里木古因诗歌和对社会问题的关注获得了来自加州大学和旧金山州立大学颁发的各种奖项，她目前是旧金山第二位桂冠诗人。

美里木古作品中反复出现的主题是美国日裔拘留营经历、这一经历给二世造成的创伤、二世对自己拘留营经历保持沉默以及抗议种族不平，等等。二世父母由于各种原因不愿意谈论或面对他们战时的拘留营经历，这让他们的三世孩子/诗人有了更加坚定的决心打破这种沉默。《在河中醒来》诗集中许多诗歌都表现了这一主题，其中"醒来"一词被用来帮助唤醒民族和政治意识。《抛弃沉默》

延续了这一重要主题,即打破关于第二次世界大战期间美国政府虐待日裔的沉默、消除针对美国亚裔女性的刻板印象,以及摆脱有辱人格的刻板印象。《危险的我们》则主要表现了美里木古的政治激进主义思想。诗人明确表达了对女性问题、与性有关的暴力以及战争的毁灭性影响——从第二次世界大战到越南战争,再到20世纪90年代初的海湾战争——的关注。

选文为《在河中醒来》诗集中的同名诗歌,描述了日裔在拘留营中的生活。

作品选读

Awake in the River

Awake in the River

The desert place. The child knew no other home.

The tortoise crawls in the hot sun. The special sun, like imprisoned, never seeming to move over the flat, flat land. Darkness falls suddenly like a velvet cloth. With it the cold, when the tortoise sleeps.

The child ran barefoot all the time, digging her toes deep into the sand, like a clawed reptile. Unlike them, she could not go beyond the barbed wire.

> Sleep,
> her mother sang,
> the sun will sap
> blood through your pores
> and make you weak.
> Sleep
> in the desert.

When the soldiers came each day, jaws like iron, picking up the men to take them to distant potato fields, she would run after her grandfather, sitting in the back of the army truck with the others, silent. Teeth gripped. Swallowing rage. Her small legs barely would reach the gate as the truck disappeared through the dust.

> Rebellion

> waits outside the gate,
> slowly gathering
> like sounds of angry snowgeese
> or water from the mountain
> springing free.
> Ocean's throat
> calls the awakening.

The children found the tortoise, big, dull shelled, making a slow journey through the desert. They named it Muhon-nin because it would not retreat into its shell, put it in the garden the men had grown from stones and succulents. Making beauty from adversity.

Old men would carve from dead wood in the shade of barracks, resurrecting images of fierce .... Women made feasts from rations to feed strength. Weaving songs with hidden messages.

> Nenneko, nenneko ya   sleep, little one
> nashite naku yara   why do you cry?

Let the tortoise go, the women would say. It is wrong to imprison any living thing.

> Kodomo ga   children
> nemutte iru   sleeping
>   frozen time
>   entombs the race
>   when will we wake?

The child, always digging, stepped deep onto a nail. Blood pouring from the bottom of her body. Mother in fear, whispering... For those who do not feign sleep, a strange life will follow. Turmoil threatens. Freedom's still a distant harvest.

The tortoise escaped. The children wept.

> Kame kame   Tortoise takes
> nigeru wa   each step
>   inevitable as time
>   full with spawn,
>   a new age

>   to the shore
>   where it will bury eggs.

Her mother washed her feet each day. The child slept, knowing she would run under another sky.

>   Born in the desert
>   cord knotted to woman/belly
>   by barbed wire.
>   Womb blazing
>   Beyond bondage.
>   The sun spreads
>   in the sand
>   touching the lip
>   of the sea,
>   rising.

The men kept their war inside. Pulling weeds by roots. Figures bent, not broken, wind rounding their backs. Grandfather wears his wait like a shell. Sleep in the desert, he warned.

>   Tortoise, empty,
>   worn,
>   plunges to the deep.
>   In the steady
>   pounding of the waves,
>   offsprings wake.

Mother steady singing by the crib.

>   Sleep in the desert.
>   Awake in the river.

18

(Florence Ai Ogawa, 1947—2010)
弗罗伦斯·爱·小川

作者简介

  弗劳伦斯·爱·小川（Florence Ai Ogawa，1947—2010）是一位拥有非裔血统的美国日裔诗人，出生于得克萨斯州奥尔巴尼（Albany, Texas），在亚利桑那州的图森（Tucson, Arizona）长大。小川在图森完成高中学业后，进入亚利桑那大学（University of Arizona）并获得了英语和东方研究的学士学位。1971年，她在加州大学欧文分校（University of California at Irvine）获得硕士学位。其间，小川几次改变她的姓氏，直到她正式用她生父的日本名字"小川"和"爱"作为她的笔名。1973年，小川出版了她的第一本诗集《残酷》（Cruelty）。此后从1979年到1999年间的20年中，她出版了6本诗集：《屠宰场》（Killing Floor, 1979）、《原罪》（Sin, 1986）、《残酷/屠宰场》（Cruelty/Killing Floor, 1987）、《命运：新诗》（Fate: New Poems, 1991）、《贪婪》（Greed, 1991）以及《堕落：新诗及精选》（Vice: New and Selected Poems, 1999）。小川获得了众多奖项：1975年获得古根海姆和邦廷基金会的奖学金、1978年获得美国国家艺术基金会的奖学金、1983年获得英格拉姆－美林基金会的奖学金等。1999年，她凭借《堕落》获得了美国国家诗歌图书奖。

  小川的诗歌经常采用独白的形式，由各种各样的人物朗诵。例如，在《残酷》中，演讲者通常是普通的匿名女性，她们受到残酷的打击，身处不幸的环境，成为幻灭和绝望的受害者。然而，在她的第二本诗集《屠宰场》中，大多数演讲者都变成著名的历史人物，作者通过他们之口来讲述生活中的悲伤与成功。《原罪》用著名和匿名角色来进行戏剧性的独白，探讨权力和性等主题。《命运》和《贪婪》

中的诗歌回归到使用著名历史人物探索社会的罪恶和邪恶。《堕落》中的作品又一次触及了美国社会的道德败坏。节选部分为诗歌《屠宰场》，作者以第一人称的形式叙述了苏联革命家托洛茨基在流亡墨西哥期间被好友杀害的故事。

作品选读

Killing Floor

1. Russia, 1927

On the day the sienna-skinned man
held my shoulders between his spade-shaped hands,
easing me down into the azure water of Jordan,
I woke ninety-three million miles from myself,
Lev Davidovich Bronstein,
shoulder-deep in the Volga,
while the cheap dye of my black silk shirt darkened the water.

My head wet, water caught in my lashes.
Am I blind?
I rub my eyes, then wade back to shore,
undress and lie down,
until Stalin comes from his place beneath the birch tree.
He folds my clothes
and I button myself in my marmot coat,
and together we start the long walk back to Moscow.
He doesn't ask, *what did you see in the river*?
but I hear the hosts of a man drowning in water and holiness,
the castrati voices I can't recognize,
skating on knives, from trees, from air
on the thin ice of my last night in Russia.
Leon Trotsky. Bread.
I want to scream, but silence holds my tongue

with small spade-shaped hands
and only this comes, so quietly

Stalin has to press his ear to my mouth:
I have only myself. Put me on the train.
I won't look back.

2. Mexico, 1940

At noon today, I woke from a nightmare:
my friend Jacques ran toward me with an ax,
as I stepped from the train in Alma-Ata.
He was dressed in yellow satin pants and shirt.
A marigold in winter.

When I held out my arms to embrace him,
he raised the ax and struck me at the neck,
my head fell to one side, hanging only by skin.
A river of sighs poured from the cut.

3. Mexico, August 20, 1940

The machine-gun bullets
hit my wife in the legs,
then zigzagged up her body.
I took the shears, cut open her gown
and lay on top of her for hours.
Blood soaked through my clothes
and when I tried to rise, I couldn't.
I wake then. Another nightmare.
I rise from my desk, walk to the bedroom
and sit down at my wife's mirrored vanity.
I rouge my cheeks and lips,
stare at my bone-white, speckled egg of a face:
lined and empty.

I lean forward and see Jacques's reflection.
I half-turn, smile, then turn back to the mirror.
He moves from the doorway,
lifts the pickax
and strikes the top of my head.
My brain splits.
The pickax keeps going
and when it hits the tile floor,
it flies from his hands,
a black dove on whose back I ride,
two men, one cursing,
the other blessing all things:
Lev Davidovich Bronstein,
I step from Jordan without you.

19
(Karen Tei Yamashita, 1951—)
山下凯伦

作者简介

山下凯伦（Karen Tei Yamashita，1951— ）是三世美国日裔作家的杰出代表。她出生于加州奥克兰，在加州大学圣克鲁兹分校（University of California, Santa Cruz）教授创意写作和美国亚裔文学，写作风格以魔幻现实主义以及后现代主义见长。美国多家主流媒体如《洛杉矶时报》、《纽约时报》以及《华盛顿新闻报》等都称赞她的写作才能以及作品所关注的主题。她的创作体裁多样，在小说、剧作、散文等方面都有建树，其中成就最大的是小说。山下迄今为止已经出版了五部小说：《穿越雨林之弧》（*Through the Arc of the Rain Forest*, 1990）、《巴西丸》（*Brazil-Maru*, 1992）、《橘子回归线》（*Tropic of Orange*, 1997）、《K 圈循环》（*Circle K Cycles*, 2001）、《I-旅馆》（*I-Hotel*, 2010），一部回忆录：《给记忆的信》（*Letters to Memory*, 2017），三部舞台剧：《征兆：一个美国歌舞伎》（*Omen: An American Kabuki*, 1976）、《广岛热带》（*Hiroshima Tropical*, 1983）、《九世：濒危物种》（*Kusei: Endangered Species*, 1986），一部短篇小说：《朝香宫》（*Asaka no Miya*, 1984），以及一部收录了她早期作品的剧作集《黄柳霜：表演的小说》（*Anime Wong: Fictions of Performance*, 2014）等。山下的作品获奖很多，她的第一部小说《穿越雨林之弧》获得了美国图书奖（American Book Award, 1991）以及珍妮特·海丁格尔·卡夫卡奖（Janet Heidinger Kafka Award, 1990），小说《I-旅馆》也进入了 2010 年美国国家图书奖（National Book Award）的决选名单。山下在小说中运用了很多后现代的写作技巧，如碎片、拼贴、杂糅、戏仿等等，同时她的小说也不局限于叙述美国日裔在美国本土的故事，而是扩展到整个世界的范围，探讨与整个人类都息息相关的议题。

《巴西丸》是一部描写1925年日本人移民巴西的小说。小说取材自山下凯伦在巴西开展田野调查所搜集的历史资料，讲述了主人公寺田一郎（Ichiro Terada）与宇野勘太郎（Kantaro Uno）、奥村（Okumura）家族等600余人，一道乘坐"巴西丸号"商船，移民到巴西，试图在一个名为埃斯波兰萨（Esperanca）的地区创建家园，却又逐渐经历家园分裂，直至最后衰败的故事。《巴西丸》描写的对象聚焦于迁往巴西的日本移民群体，较为详细地探讨了整个族群的生活境况，并且在布局上直接以史料入文，采用虚构与真实相结合的手法，将虚构的人物与真实的历史糅合在一起。节选部分为《巴西丸》第一章，描写乘船前往巴西的日本人初到巴西的见闻与感受。

作品选读

Brazil-Maru

Chapter 1
Brazil-Maru
(Excerpt)

It was 1925. São Paulo, Brazil. I stuck my head out the window, straining to see the beginning and the end of the train as it chugged slowly up the side of the mountain. The tepid heat of the port of Santos below rose around us in a soft cloud that silently engulfed my view of the now distant port and the ship and the shimmering ocean beyond. The creeping altitude and the rocking train seemed to lull the minds of the passengers so recently stunned by our first impressions. I had seen it myself from the ship below—the sheer green wall lifting into a mass of shifting clouds, daring us to scale it.

How many other Japanese immigrants had already witnessed this scene? Since 1908, they had arrived at this same port in shipload after shipload until there were thousands of Japanese, the majority laboring on coffee plantations in the state of São Paulo.

I had stumbled down the gangway clutching a bundle entrusted to me. My mother was carrying little Yōzo on her back. Eiji clutched her dress with one hand, and Hiro held on to Eiji. My father lumbered down with our heavy bags. Although I was only nine years old, I was still the oldest and had to take care of myself. I saw the scholar Shūhei Mizuoka already on the dock struggling with his bags loaded with books. For a moment I sensed a need to look back at the ship we were leaving, and there at the top of the plank was Grandma Uno still standing transfixed, staring at this idea we all had traveled so far to see, this Brazil.

Below, dockworkers pushed loaded carts or trudged under heavy sacks, their soiled shirts patched with circles of sweat. It was not the first time I had seen people of other colors and features. We had followed a route around the earth, sailing south from Japan through the South China Sea to Singapore, then on to Ceylon and the Cape of Good Hope; the ship had docked on the coast of India and the tip of Africa, but still I stared as the ship traded its human cargo for coffee and bananas.

The din of this activity pitched about us, but we were oddly silent, dumbfounded upon seeing what two months of dreams aboard a plodding ship upon the sea had brought. The dank humidity pressed upon us. I saw Grandma Uno's shoulders stoop; perhaps her old heart hesitated. Her grandson Kantaro nudged her at her elbow. "What is it?" he asked. She looked up at him, so tall and handsome and so anxious to step onto this land.

"Ichiro!" my mother called back to me. I hurried on, but not before I saw Grandma Uno push Kantaro aside and walk purposely down alone to land.

We had borne the heavy humidity of the port of Santos along with all our worldly possessions from the ship to the waiting train, and now we were climbing upward with our burdens, struggling against our better senses to gain the plateau. There was some relief as we climbed; the shadowed air filtered through the dense vegetation but so did the smell. We had traded the salty taste of the sea and the fragrance of coffee and bananas for this other smell. It had flooded the car somewhere below us as we passed through what seemed to be a black swamp of rotting vegetation that had dropped off in disintegrating pieces from the great green wall. We had captured the odor of that putrid rot within the confines of the rocking train. I had not felt seasick those many days at sea, but now suddenly I was overcome with nausea.

For many hours the train plodded upward through the green wall. Occasionally we passed through a tunnel, but it did not seem to clear the air. I struggled with my discomfort until it passed into a kind of dream. Flitting through the green wall and mist,

I saw a fox, a horned devil, a white-faced ghost, the monsters of my childhood. And then, they were gone forever as the train emerged onto a plateau, and the land stretched out for miles into the distant horizon—pastures of grazing zebu, fields of corn, coffee, and sugarcane spotted by thick patches of the old tangled forest and sweeping mango and avocado trees, and only occasionally disturbed by a lonely brick or mud-thatched cottage—a land spacious and vast, and all so different from Japan.

"Well, Ichiro," my father said. "What do you think? It's beyond my imagination," my father answered himself. "So here we are." We looked around at my brothers huddled around and in my mother's lap. They were all sleeping in a big heap. My father looked at me and smiled, "Ichiro, somehow I knew you'd be awake for this."

The train came to a stop at what seemed to be a rural way station. It was also a marketplace of sorts. Vendors sat with their produce spread on mats or makeshift stands. A few peddlers ran along the train shouting through the windows. They had wares in baskets: dried meats, fresh fish, cakes and sweets, strange fruits like bananas and papayas, and birds—some dead, some alive. A great wall of chickens squawked from their cages. I ran out the open door of the car, finally overcome by my sickness, and heaved the contents of my poor stomach onto the new land. My relief was sudden, but my attention was easily diverted by a boy who ran toward me chasing a squealing piglet. He caught the piglet, but it squirmed away and ran off, knocking me to the ground. It had jumped on my chest and over my head, leaving its dirty prints and sour smell behind. I felt an indescribable disgust and joy all at once urging me to join the boy in his chase, scurrying after the slippery pig and running toward that great wall of chickens. Just as it was about to slip between the cages, I dove upon the squealing pig, pinning it beneath my chest. I looked up at cages teetering above to see the face of the pig's young owner, a mixture of relief and gratitude and comedy glowing in his features. For a short moment that boy and I were locked in some middle space where our two curious minds stared at the unknown.

I remember that face as if it were yesterday, the golden sun-bleached burnish at the tips of his curly brown hair, the dark olive skin beneath a healthy glow of sweat, the richness of his deep brown eyes. The boy spoke in a language I could not understand, and yet, I was sure from that moment on that I would soon understand everything. Over the years, I have thought from time to time that I had caught a glimpse of that very boy again, but of course, it could never be the same boy. If he is indeed alive today, he must be, like me, another old man with memories.

◇ ◇ ◇

There were six of us in my family in 1925 when we arrived in Brazil—my father, Kiyoshi Terada; my mother, Sei; and my three younger brothers. As I said, I was the oldest son, although only nine years old. My mother was pregnant when we arrived in Brazil. Everyone spoke about her next child as being doubtless a girl, that so drastic a change in our lives on this earth would surely change the pattern, but this did not happen. Interesting to recall that with all the changes of place and fortune, some things did *not* change, and it was finally expected that my mother would always give birth to boys.

My family was originally from the town of Matsumoto in the mountains of Nagano Prefecture in central Japan. My father came from a family of pharmacists, and he too had a license. My mother, who was actually a second cousin to my father, was a trained midwife. Their marriage must have seemed a logical one to their families, and there was, indeed, a quiet understanding between my parents about everything, or so it seemed to me. When Momose-sensei came to speak about starting a new life on new land in Brazil, they seemed to agree almost immediately that this was the destiny ... intended for us.

By the 1920s many Japanese, especially second sons without rights of inheritance, had left to find a livelihood abroad. We knew of several men from our town who had left for California at the turn of the century. My mother knew the fish market family whose oldest sister had left to join her husband in San Francisco. But that was the last anyone had heard or seen of these people. By the time I was born, these stories seemed like the distant past. And yet, every year more and more poor tenant farmers who complained of high taxes and no future looked for opportunities far away. The recent Kanto earthquake of 1923 had left many homeless and unemployed. In cities and towns, students were unable to find work after their schooling, and strikes were rampant among the urban industries. Now my parents discussed their plans to leave too. Everyone came to share their thoughts on the matter.

"Momose-sensei's lived in America, but he was very clear in his meaning. He said our future is in Brazil."

People remembered the 1918 Rice Rebellion when twenty-five thousand peasants protested the high price of rice. This and pro-communist and proletariat movements later provoked government repression. For people like my parents, educated Christians with socialist sentiments, Brazil would be a new beginning.

"Anyway, we've missed our chance to go to America now. The Americans signed an Exclusion Act that won't allow us in."

"I heard that most of Brazil is virgin forest, not like America at all. Brazil is looking for people to develop the country."

"What about those ads calling for contract laborers to harvest Brazilian coffee?"

"This is different. We won't be contract labor. We'll have our own land from the very beginning. Momose-sensei has arranged for a concession from the state of São Paulo. We saw the maps and the allocation of the lots."

"Imagine, sixty acres of land for one family! How much land is that? More than an entire village, and then there are two hundred such lots available—more than 120,000 acres!"

"And," my father confided to his closest friends, "there will be others like us. Christians with the same convictions. We will be able to create a new civilization."

A new civilization. This perhaps sounds strange today, but in those early years, that is the way we used to talk about colonizing Brazil, especially about the particular Japanese colony located on the far northwestern corner of the state of São Paulo, founded by the Christian evangelist, Momose-sensei, and where my parents chose lot number thirty-three: Esperanga.

❁ ❁ ❁

We left Japan from the port of Kobe on a ship named the *Brazil-maru*. The voyage on the *Brazil-maru* lasted some sixty days. Most of the six hundred emigrants on the ship were going to Brazil as contract laborers to work on coffee plantations, hired on by the Imperial Immigration Company. The Brazilian government required that contract labor enter Brazil in family units, but this was not always how things worked out. Unknown to government authorities, immigrants, when necessary, created family units, oftentimes mixing and matching relatives and friends and strangers.

For example, I met a boy named Kōji on the ship who was borrowed by his bachelor uncle to complete a family unit. And Kōji confided to me that the woman who was traveling with them was not his mother; she was a stranger from another village. In the beginning, she was mostly seasick, and her eyes were always red from crying. I heard my mother say that this woman was running away because she did not want to marry the man her family had chosen for her. My mother, being a midwife, naturally met many women on the ship and heard the gossip. She also went to comfort this woman.

"I've made a terrible mistake. I didn't realize how far away Brazil is," she sobbed to my mother.

"You must make the best of this situation," my mother said. "What about the poor boy? He's not your own, but he's only a child. He doesn't say so, but he's probably as homesick and afraid as you are." I didn't think much of Kōji's situation then, but now I wonder what ever became of him. He was not much older than I.

My family was different from the other Japanese on the ship. We had paid for our passage and were destined to settle land we had bought, while the contract laborers were committed to several years of labor to pay for their passage. But we were all alike in our expectations of Brazil: the promised wealth of the coffee harvest, the vastness of the land, the adventure of a new life. And I think most of the immigrants were alike in thinking that they would return—after their contracts were up or in a few years, however long it might take—to Japan with certain wealth, stories of adventure, and the pride of success. I believe my parents thought that surely they would see their homeland and their families in Nagano once again, at least to visit. As we watched the port of Kobe disappear on the ocean's horizon, I thought *I* would return. But my father said to me, as I turned with the others on the deck, "Ichiro, we're going to a new country, a new life. Everything begins from this moment. Don't look back." I think my father knew I would never return. He did not believe, like so many did, that Japan was the only place in the world to live.

From that moment, my memories of Japan faded; visions of my birthplace became to me a blur. And yet, I have a very clear memory of everything from that moment on: the movement of the ship upon the sea, the snap of cards and the laughter of men gambling, the banter of immigrant talk in different dialects, quarrels with my brothers and our tireless exploration of every nook and cranny in the ship—and the camera.

20

(Philip Kan Gotanda, 1951—)
菲利普·菅·五反田

作者简介

菲利普·菅·五反田（Philip Kan Gotanda, 1951— ）是一名三世美国日裔剧作家和编剧。他出生在加州斯托克顿，父亲在第二次世界大战期间被强制拘禁在阿肯色州的罗厄集中营（Rohwer Camp, Arkansas）。五反田在加州大学圣克鲁斯分校学习了一年之后，离开美国到日本学习陶瓷技术，之后于1973年在加州大学圣芭芭拉分校完成了日本艺术学位。尽管他对艺术、音乐和剧本创作都有兴趣，但他还是在1978年获得了黑斯廷斯法学院的学位。五反田对剧本创作一直保持着兴趣，他与美国亚裔著名剧作家赵健秀、黄哲伦有着亲密的关系。五反田的戏剧作品包括《北村之梦》（*The Dream of Kitamura*, 1983）、《清洁》（*The Wash*, 1987）、《鱼头汤》（*Fish Head Soup*, 1995）、《二世渔夫之歌》（*A Song for a Nisei Fisherman*, 1995）、《美国佬，你死定了》（*Yankee Dawg You Die*, 1991）、《松本姐妹》（*Sisters Matsumoto*, 1997）和《漂浮的野草》（*Floating Weeds*, 2000）等。五反田曾获得古根海姆、麦克奈特、美国国家艺术基金会和洛克菲勒基金会的奖学金，以及皮尤慈善信托和戏剧交流组织颁发的美国艺术家奖（National Artist Award from the PEW Charitable Trust and Theatre Communications group）和莱拉·华莱士读者文摘作家奖（Lila Wallace-Reader's Digest Writer's Award）。

五反田的戏剧《美国佬，你死定了》探索的中心目标是种族主义。这部剧不像五反田的其他作品那样只关注美国日裔；相反，它呈现了整个美国亚裔群体所经历的种族主义和种族刻板印象。这部剧跨越了种族——两个主要角色，文森特·张（Vincent Chang）和布拉德利·山下（Bradley Yamashita）分别是美国华裔和日裔；跨越了代际——张和山下是不同的世代，探讨美国亚裔社区的婚恋观问题并批评美国种族主义政策。这些交织在一起的因素在娱乐行业中得到体现，美国亚裔演员在挣扎于他们的种族和性别身份的同时，也与主流媒体在舞台上对他们的描述和台下的刻板印象作斗争。下文节选部分是本剧的第一幕第三场，张与山下二人讨论亚裔在好莱坞受到的歧视。

作品选读

Yankee Dawg You Die

Scene Three

"THEY EDITED IT OUT"
After an acting class. Vincent is upset. Bradley packing his duffle bag.

VINCENT: You do not know a thing about the industry. Not a damn thing. Who the hell …

BRADLEY: (*Interrupts, calling to someone across the room*) Yeah, Alice—I'll get my lines down for our scene, sorry.

VINCENT: (*Attempts to lower his voice so as not to be heard*) Who the hell are you to talk to me that way. Been in the business a few…

BRADLEY: (*Interrupts*) Look, if I offended you last time by something I said, I'm sorry. I like your work, Mr. Chang. You know that. I like your…

VINCENT: (*Interrupts*) A "Chinese Steppin Fetchit"—that is what you called me. A "Chinese Steppin Fetchit." Remember?

BRADLEY: I'm an angel, OK, I'm an angel. *No memory.*

VINCENT: And you do not belong in this class.

BRADLEY: My agent at William Morris arranged for me to join this class.

VINCENT: This is for *advanced* actors.

BRADLEY: I've been acting in the theatre for seven years, Mr. Chang.

VINCENT: Seven years? Seven years? Seven years is a wink of an eye. An itch on the ass. A fart in my sleep, my fine feathered friend.

BRADLEY: I've been acting at the Theatre Project of Asian America in San Francisco for seven years—acting, directing, writing…

VINCENT: Poppycock, cockypoop, bullshit. Theatre Project of Asian America—"Amateur Hour."

BRADLEY: "Amateur Hour?" Asian American theatres are where we do the real work, Mr. Chang.

VINCENT: The business, Bradley, I am talking about the business, the industry. That Matthew Iwasaki movie was a fluke, an accident...

BRADLEY: (*Interrupts*) Film, Mr. Chang.

VINCENT: *Movie*! And stop calling me Mr. Chang. It's Shigeo Nakada. "Asian American consciousness." Hah. You can't even tell the difference between a Chinaman and a Jap. I'm Japanese, didn't you know that? I changed my name after the war. Hell, I wanted to work...

BRADLEY: (*Mutters*) You are so jive, Mr. Chang...

VINCENT: You think you're better than I, don't you? Somehow special, above it all. The new generation. With all your fancy politics about this Asian American new-way-of-thinking and seven long years of paying your dues at Asian Project Theatre or whatever it is. You don't know shit my friend. You don't know the meaning of paying your dues in this business.

BRADLEY: The business. You keep talking about the business. The industry. Hollywood. What's Hollywood? Cutting up your face to look more white? So my nose is a little flat. Fine! Flat is beautiful. So I don't have a double-fold in my eyelid. Great! No one in my entire racial family has had it in the last 10,000 years. My old girlfriend used to put scotch tape on her eyelids to get the double fold so she could look more "Cau-ca-sian." My new girlfriend—she doesn't mess around, she got surgery. Where does it begin? Vincent? All that self hate, *where does it begin*? You and your Charley Chop Suey roles...

VINCENT: You want to know the truth? I'm glad I did it. Yes, you heard me right. I'm glad I did it and I'm not ashamed, I wanted to do it. And no one is ever going to get an apology out of me. And in some small way it is a victory. Yes, a victory. At least an Oriental was on screen acting, being seen. We existed.

BRADLEY: But that's not existing—wearing some goddamn monkey suit and kissing up to some white man, that's not existing.

VINCENT: That's all there was, Bradley. That's all there was! But you don't think I wouldn't have wanted to play a better role than that bucktoothed, groveling waiter? I would have killed for a better role where I could have played an honest-to-... human being with real emotions. I would have killed for it. You seem to assume "Asian Americans" always existed. That there were always roles for you. You didn't exist back then buster. Back then there was no Asian American consciousness, no Asian American actor, and no Asian American theatres. Just a handful of "Orientals" who for some ...-forsaken reason wanted to perform. *Act.* And we did. At church bazaars, community talent night, and on the Chop Suey Circuit playing China-towns and Little Tokyos around the country as hoofers, jugglers, acrobats, strippers—anything we could for anyone who would watch. You, you with that holier-than-thou look, trying to make me feel ashamed. You wouldn't be here if it weren't for all the crap we had put up with. We built something. We built the mountain, as small as it may be, that you stand on so proudly looking down at me. Sure, it's a mountain of Charley Chop Suey's and slipper-toting geishas. But it is also filled with forgotten moments of extraordinary wonder, artistic achievement. A singer, Larry Ching, he could croon like Frank Sinatra and better looking, too. Ever heard of him? Toy Yet Mar—boy, she could belt it out with the best of them. "The Chinese Sophie Tucker." No one's ever heard of her. And Dorothy Takahashi, she could dance the high heels off of anyone, Ginger Rodgers included. And, who in the hell has ever heard of Fred Astaire and Dorothy Takahashi? Dead dreams, my friend. Dead dreams, broken backs and long forgotten beauty. I swear sometimes when I'm taking my curtain call I can see this shadowy figure out of the corner of my eye taking the most glorious, dignified bow. *Who* remembers? Who appreciates?

BRADLEY: See, you think every time you do one of those demeaning roles, the only thing lost is *your* dignity. That the only person who has to pay is you. Don't you see that every time you do that millions of people in movie theaters will see it. Believe it. Every time you do any old stereotypic role just to pay the bills, someone has to pay for it—and it ain't you. *No.* It's some Asian kid innocently walking home. "Hey, it's a Chinaman gook!" "Rambo, Rambo, Rambo!?" You older actors. You ask to be understood, forgiven, but you refuse to change. You have no sense of social responsibility. Only me...

VINCENT: (*Overlapping*) No...

BRADLEY: ... me, me. Shame on you. I'd never play a role like that stupid waiter in that musical. And...

VINCENT: You don't know...

BRADLEY: ... I'd never let them put so much makeup on my face that I look like some goddamn chimpanzee on the screen.

VINCENT: (*Overlapping*) You don't know ...

BRADLEY: I don't care if they paid me a million dollars, what good is it to lose your dignity. I'm not going to prostitute my soul just to…

VINCENT: (*Overlapping*) There's that word. I was wondering when we'd get around to that word. I hate that word! I HATE THAT WORD!

BRADLEY: … see myself on screen if I have to go grunting around like some slant-eyed animal. You probably wouldn't know a good role if it grabbed you by the balls!

VINCENT: I have played many good roles.

BRADLEY: Sure, waiters, Viet Cong killers, chimpanzees, drug dealers, hookers…

VINCENT: (*Interrupts*) I was the first to be nominated for an Academy Award.

BRADLEY: Oh, it's pull-out-the-old-credits time. But what about some of the TV stuff you've been doing lately. Jesus, TV! At least in the movies we're still dangerous. But TV? They fucking cut off our balls and made us all house boys on the evening soaps. (*Calls out*) "Get your very own neutered, Oriental houseboy!"

VINCENT: I got the woman once. (*Bradley doesn't understand*) In the movie. I got the woman.

BRADLEY: Sure.

VINCENT: And she was *white*.

BRADLEY: You're so full of it.

VINCENT: And I kissed her!

BRADLEY: What, a peck on the cheek?

VINCENT: ON THE LIPS! ON THE LIPS! *I GOT THE WOMAN.*

BRADLEY: Nah.

VINCENT: Yes.

BRADLEY: Nah?

VINCENT: YES.

BRADLEY: (*Pondering*) When was this? In the '30s. Before the war?

VINCENT: (*Overlapping*) No.

BRADLEY: Because that happened back then. After the war forget it. Mr. Moto even disappeared and he was played by Peter Lorre.

VINCENT: No, no. This was the '50s.

BRADLEY: Come on, you're kidding.

VINCENT: 1959. A cop movie. (*Correcting himself*) Film. *The Scarlet Kimono*. Directed by Sam Fuller. Set in L.A. Two police detectives, one Japanese American and one Caucasian. And a beautiful blond, they both love.

BRADLEY: Yeah ... I remember. And there's this violent kendo fight between you two guys because you both want the woman. (*Realizing*) And you get the woman.

VINCENT: See, I told you so. (*Pause. Bradley seated himself*)

BRADLEY: Except when I saw it you didn't kiss her. I mean I would have remembered something like that. An Asian man and a white woman. You didn't kiss her.

VINCENT: TV?

BRADLEY: Late Night. (*Bradley nods. Vincent making the realization*)

VINCENT: They edited it out. (*Silence. Vincent is upset. Bradley watches him. Dim to darkness*)

21

(Garrett Hongo, 1951—)
加利特·本乡

作者简介

加利特·本乡（Garrett Hongo, 1951— ）是一名美国日裔诗人和回忆录作家，出生在夏威夷火山村（Volcano, Hawaii），他的回忆录就是以自己出生的村庄命名。六岁时，本乡随家人搬到了洛杉矶，体验了他在夏威夷没有接触过的城市生活。本乡1973年获得英语学士学位后在日本度过了一年时光，并对日本文化产生了浓厚的兴趣。之后，他在西雅图待了几年，参与了赵健秀和劳森·稻田等人的美国亚裔文学运动，并成立了一个名为"排亚法案"（the Asian Exclusion Act）的剧团，上演了赵健秀的《龙年》以及山内若子的《灵魂将要起舞》等戏剧。

1980年，本乡回到学校，获得了加州大学欧文分校的艺术硕士学位。1982年，他出版了个人第一部文集《黄光》（*Yellow Light*），随后又出版了《天河》（*The River of Heaven*, 1988）。1995年，他出版了个人自传作品《火山：夏威夷回忆录》（*Volcano: A Memoir of Hawai'i*）。本乡获得过许多奖项和奖学金：发现/国家奖（Discovery/The Nation Award）、拉蒙特诗歌奖（Lamont Poetry Prize）、俄勒冈非小说类图书奖（Oregon Book Award in Non-Fiction）、古根海姆奖学金、洛克菲勒基金会驻院奖学金（Rockefeller Foundation Residency Fellowship）、两次国家艺术基金会奖学金（National Endowment for the Arts Fellowships），并在1989年获得普利策奖提名。

本乡的很多诗歌都关注美国亚裔历史和文化，尤其是亚裔在美国的沉默。他的回忆录《火山》聚焦于"家"与"家园"的概念，回顾了诗人在夏威夷地方文化中的经历，将真实和想象中的人物联系在一起，充满了浓浓的乡愁。作为一部回忆录同时也是美国日裔家庭编年史以及自然史的辉煌之作,《火山》讲述了本乡年轻时回到出生地夏威夷,重拾梦幻般的风景和自己难以捉摸的过去时所发生的事情。他通过具体化他个人和家庭的历史来关注文化和民族遗产、风景,并回应故乡遗产和地方的召唤。节选部分叙述本乡的父亲去世之后,作者回忆父母过往的生活经历。

作品选读

Volcano: A Memoir of Hawai'i

Dragon

  My father died in a poor Los Angeles hospital gasping for breath, his heart already stopped. He was getting tucked into his remade bed in intensive care, telling the cheery Filipino nurse, who had just told him the mini-chronicle of her move from Manila, that he was a wanderer too, when his heart, which had been racing all day without steadiness, which had suffered some inconsolable damage, simply quit on him in mid-sentence. One instant he was saying, quietly, with deliberation and in the normal rhythms of exchange, that he was from Hawaii, and in the immediate next, with no prefatory remark or transition, he was panicked, saying that he couldn't breathe. Death had slipped itself into his body that swiftly. Within seconds he passed—the heart monitor had already beeped—and everything else went into flatline. A doctor came and administered the drill, sustaining it for nearly twenty minutes, but my father was gone.

  He'd been ill for nearly a week. He came home from his night shift job in Santa Monica with intense pains in his chest, falling through the front door of his house, calling out loud for my mother, who was far back in the bedroom of the tract home, sleeping. She told me he was sitting down on the gray carpet by the entry way, breathing hard, pumping his arm, balling his fist again and again, already rising, trying to stand. She thought he was drunk and had passed out on the floor. She worried he would vomit. She argued with him, spewing out rebukes, until she realized how serious things were and called the paramedics. They too thought he was just drunk—and he had been, downing a huge dose of Yukon Jack while he sat in his car in the parking lot of his working place before driving home around midnight.

He'd been fighting with his bosses, arguing about the way to do things, about the way he'd done things years before on some instruments he'd built for a helicopter control panel. The unit had come back on guarantee, and no one in the factory could fix it except my father. The boards under the dials didn't conform to specs, so it fell to my father, a senior troubleshooter, to devise how to repair it. But there were no plans, no handbook or electronic blueprints to work from. He'd have to improvise, do lots of checking, take time and do shitwork in order to get it done. He was being punished for screwing up. He had been given work that was obviously humiliating, and the bosses had rebuked him for objecting. In front of everyone. Someone had laughed. Most were silenced by the pub-lie dressing-down, embarrassed for him, an "old-timer" with the company, helplessly waiting out his pension. My father had gotten angry, and stalked off, fuming in Hawaiian pidgin English—his only language. Hard-of-hearing since childhood, language and speech came with difficulty to him, so he befriended others who also spoke differently. But even his cohorts on the job—nonunionized Chicanos, southern blacks, Thais and Cambodians, a Native American who asked him deer-hunting every year—had ignored or mocked him, ostracizing him further, fearful of being allied, of being marked for firing, as he certainly was.

He was only five years from retirement, maybe two if he'd decided to take it early, and the company was probably trying to force him out, make him quit early and save a little on the payments, encouraging him to move out before the big payday. They wanted him out—that seemed certain—and they chose to bust him down in front of the boys in order to motivate him to make a move. With executives, companies act high-minded and give them a golden handshake. With factory workers, they parcel out scorn and ridicule, layoffs and dismissals. So, my father got angry one night after a meeting with his boss and stalked away, grabbing up the little red pack of his shirt-pocket tool kit, walking across the factory floor, kicking a plastic trash can, scraping the legs of his metal stool across the concrete floor when he sat down and hunkered over his drafting table, awakened to his own expendability.

Was he being fired? I never found out. My mother drew a silence down on all of it. It was another secret she drew over his life, like the huge one over our beginnings.

If ever I asked her about any of these—about the death of my father, about our lives in Hawaii, about my Hongo grandparents—I'd get evasive or silly answers, a switch in subject. I wasn't to know. During childhood and adolescence, it was no hard thing to silence questions and stifle curiosity with small bits of fact—"Your Hongo grandfather was a tall man…" "Your dad used to work construction for the military..." "Your relatives on the Big Island grow orchids…" "Your Uncle Torakiyo lost all his property in a tidal wave..." But if I probed deeper, if I wanted the telling to continue, I was cut off with impatience, with mocking, or with anger. Her sister and my uncle, who lived near us in Los Angeles, who shared holidays with us, would shush me too. My mother was bothered by these things. She would not let me know but the barest sketches of the past. Until I was past thirty, I was allowed nothing of simple family knowledge. And, for over thirty years, little curiosity had risen within me. But after the funeral, after I had buried my father who had come from such faint and unknown beginnings, I felt the deepest shame that would not be buried with his ashes. After my father's death, family secrets, evasions, and my own ignorance fed an anger and a desire to know that would not abate.

I remember paging furiously through the newspaper the day after he died, looking for the weather report, needing to prepare some distracting fragment of information to give to his sisters in Hawaii when I called them. At the end of the Sports section, on the page where regional and national temperatures are printed, where the barometric lows and highs ran, where the moon phases and tidal charts were given, was a satellite picture of the Los Angeles basin on the day before. There had been a terrible Santa Ana storm—desert winds blowing in from the east and across the mountains—a day in which the normal onshore patterns were powerfully reversed. A merciless continuum of hot, desiccating, blasting air had scoured through from the canyons down across the flatlands and out toward sea. I remember the news reports of gusts up to eighty miles per hour in the Anaheim Hills. Dust and trash kicked up, Dumpsters clanged and banged their lids, eucalyptus and jacaranda trees had their limbs sheared off, and streetlights suspended over traffic bounced and dandled like panicky moths caught struggling in deadly, electric webs over the intersections of the city. People got surly and turned inward. I had shielded my eyes from the dry, stinging heat slapping at me all that day. A visiting instructor at a university, I had taught my classes, driving to school in the heavy winds, feeling my tiny car bounce and swerve a little on the freeway as I drove to campus and then with my wife Cynthia to the hospital later that evening. The aerial photo showed all of this in a huge swirl of clouds over the L.A. basin. Between San Bernardino and Santa Monica, between the eastern mountains and the large bay to the west, was the white serpentine of a dragon spiraling out from my father's deathbed.

22

(Sylvia Watanabe, 1953—)
西尔维娅·渡边

作者简介

西尔维娅·渡边（Sylvia Watanabe, 1953—）是夏威夷日裔短篇小说作家。她出生于毛伊岛的威鲁库（Wailuku, Maui），在瓦胡岛的凯卢阿（Kailua, Oahu）长大。1980年她获得夏威夷大学艺术史学士学位，1985年获得纽约州立大学宾汉顿分校（State University of New York at Binghamton）英语和创意写作硕士学位。1995年，渡边在俄亥俄州奥柏林学院（Oberlin College, Ohio）找到了一份永久的教学工作。渡边于1992年出版了名为《与死者交谈：故事》（*Talking to the Dead: Stories*）的故事集，被《人物》杂志评为"十佳图书"；1993年获得笔会奥克兰分会约瑟芬·迈尔斯奖（Josephine Miles Award from the Oakland Chapter of PEN）；并入围1992—1993年笔会/福克纳小说奖（PEN/Faulkner Award for Fiction）。此外，她的一些个人故事还获得了欧·亨利奖、美国日裔公民联盟国家文学奖（Japanese American Citizens League National Literary Award）和手推车奖（Pushcart Prize）等荣誉。

夏威夷是渡边的出生地，为她的许多故事提供了灵感和背景，其中很多都是基于她对自己出生成长的毛伊岛的记忆。《与死者交谈：故事》中，渡边虚构了一个叫鲁伊（Luhi）的夏威夷海边小镇作为故事的发生地，描述了美国日裔社区以及生活在其中的一世和二世美国日裔女性。夏威夷的独特地理位置赋予了她的故事情节和主题以意义。这些故事跨越了从第二次世界大战结束到20世纪70年代之间的30年，这期间夏威夷经历了重大的经济和社会变革。这些变化反映在故事集中女性角色的生活中，包括她们的职业选择、困境，以及她们与他人和土地的关系。下文节选部分为本故事集的标题故事《与死者交谈》。作为旧生活方式的实践者，可以与死者交谈的阿姨必须找到一个继任者，以继续她的角色。小说提出了现代化对传统生活方式的挑战这一问题。

作品选读

Talking to the Dead: Stories

(Excerpt)

We spoke of her in whispers as Aunty Talking to the Dead, the half-Hawaiian kahuna lady. But whenever there was a death in the village, she was the first to be sent for—the priest came second. For it was she who understood the wholeness of things—the significance of directions and colors. Prayers to appease the hungry ghosts. Elixirs for grief. Most times, she'd be out on her front porch, already waiting—her boy, Clinton, standing behind with her basket of spells—when the messenger arrived. People said she could smell a death from clear on the other side of the island, even as the dying person breathed his last. And if she fixed her eyes on you and named a day, you were already as good as six feet under.

I went to work as her apprentice when I was eighteen. That was in '48—the year Clinton graduated from mortician school on the G.I. Bill. It was the talk for weeks—how he returned to open the Paradise Mortuary in the very heart of the village and brought the scientific spirit of free enterprise to the doorstep of the hereafter. I remember the advertisements for the Grand Opening—promising to modernize the funeral trade with Lifelike Artistic Techniques and Stringent Standards of Sanitation. The old woman, who had waited out the war for her son's return, stoically took his defection in stride and began looking for someone else to help out with her business.

At the time, I didn't have many prospects—more schooling didn't interest me, and my mother's attempts at marrying me off inevitably failed when I stood to shake hands with a prospective bridegroom and ended up towering a foot above him. "It's bad enough she has the face of a horse," I heard one of them complain.

My mother dressed me in navy blue, on the theory that dark colors make everything look smaller; "Yuri, sit down," she'd hiss, tugging at my skirt as the decisive moment approached. I'd nod, sip my tea, smile through the introductions and boring small talk, till the time came for sealing the bargain with handshakes all around. Then nothing on earth could keep me from getting to my feet. The go-between finally suggested that I consider taking up a trade. "After all, marriage isn't for everyone," she said. My mother said that that was a fact which remained to be proved, but meanwhile, it wouldn't hurt if I took in sewing or learned to cut hair. I made up my mind to apprentice myself to Aunty Talking to the Dead.

The old woman's house was on the hill behind the village, in some woods, just off the road to Chicken Fight Camp. She lived in an old plantation worker's bungalow with peeling green and white paint and a large, well-tended garden out front—mostly of flowering bushes and strong-smelling herbs I didn't know the names of.

"Aren't you a big one," a gravelly voice behind me rasped.

I started, then turned. It was the first time I had ever seen the old woman up close.

"Hello... uh... Mrs... Mrs... Dead," I stammered.

She was little—way under five feet—and wrinkled, and everything about her seemed the same color—her skin, her lips, her dress—everything just a slightly different shade of the same brown-grey, except her hair, which was absolutely white, and her tiny eyes, which glinted like metal. For a minute, those eyes looked me up and down.

"Here," she said finally, thrusting an empty rice sack into my hands. "For collecting salt." And she started down the road to the beach.

In the next few months, we walked every inch of the hills and beaches around the village, and then some.

"This is *a'ali'i* to bring sleep—it must be dried in the shade on a hot day." Aunty was always three steps ahead, chanting, while I struggled behind, laden with strips of bark and leafy twigs, my head buzzing with names.

"This is *awa* for every kind of grief, and *uhaloa* with the deep roots—if you are like that, death cannot easily take you," Her voice came from the stones, the trees, and the earth.

"This is where you gather salt to preserve a corpse," I hear her still. "This is where you cut to insert the salt," her words have marked the places on my body, one by one.

That whole first year, not a single day passed when I didn't think of quitting. I tried to figure out a way of moving back home without making it seem like I was admitting anything.

"You know what people are saying, don't you?" my mother said, lifting the lid of the bamboo steamer and setting a tray of freshly-steamed meat buns on the already-crowded table before me. It was one of the few visits home since my apprenticeship—though I'd never been more than a couple of miles away—and she had stayed up the whole night before, cooking. The kitchen table was near-overflowing—she'd prepared a canned ham with yellow sweet potatoes, wing beans with pork, sweet and sour mustard cabbage, fresh raw yellow-fin, pickled egg plant, and rice with red beans. I had not seen so much food since the night she tried to persuade her younger brother, my Uncle Mongoose, not to volunteer for the army. He went anyway, and on the last day of training, just before he was shipped to Italy, he shot himself in the head when he was cleaning his gun. "I always knew that boy would come to no good," was all Mama said when she heard the news.

"What do you mean you can't eat another bite," she fussed now. "Look at you, nothing but a bag of bones."

I allowed myself to be persuaded to another helping, though I'd lost my appetite.

The truth was, there didn't seem to be much of a future in my apprenticeship. In eleven and a half months, I had memorized most of the minor rituals of mourning and learned to identify a couple of dozen herbs and all their medicinal uses, but I had not seen—much less gotten to practice on—a single honest-to-goodness corpse.

"People live longer these days," Aunty claimed.

But I knew it was because everyone—even from villages across the bay—had begun taking their business to the Paradise Mortuary. The single event which established Clinton's monopoly once and for all was the untimely death of old Mrs. Pomadour, the plantation owner's mother-in-law, who choked on a fishbone during a fundraising luncheon of the Famine Relief Society. Clinton was chosen to be in charge of the funeral. He took to wearing three-piece suits—even during the humid Kona season—as a symbol of his new respectability, and was nominated as a Republican candidate to run for the village council.

"So, what are people saying, Mama?" I asked, finally pushing my plate away.

This was the cue she had been waiting for. "They're saying that That Woman has gotten herself a new donkey..." She paused dramatically, holding my look with her eyes. The implication was clear.

I began remembering things about being in my mother's house. The navy blue dresses. The humiliating weekly tea ceremony lessons at the Buddhist Temple.

"Give up this foolishness," she wheedled. "Mrs. Koyama tells me the Barber Shop Lady is looking for help…"

"I think I'll stay right where I am," I said.

My mother drew herself up. "Here, have another meat bun," she said, jabbing one through the center with her serving fork and lifting it onto my plate.

A few weeks later, Aunty and I were called just outside the village to perform a laying-out. It was early afternoon when Sheriff Kanoi came by to tell us that the body of Mustard Hayashi, the eldest of the Hayashi boys, had just been pulled from an irrigation ditch by a team of field workers. He had apparently fallen in the night before, stone drunk, on his way home from Hula Rose's Dance Emporium.

I began hurrying around, assembling Aunty's tools and bottles of potions, and checking that everything was in working order, but the old woman didn't turn a hair; she just sat calmly rocking back and forth and puffing on her skinny, long-stemmed pipe.

"Yuri, you stop that rattling around back there!" she snapped, then turned to the Sheriff. "My son Clinton could probably handle this. Why don't you ask him?"

"No, Aunty," Sheriff Kanoi replied. "This looks like a tough case that's going to need some real expertise."

"Mmmm…" The old woman stopped rocking. "It's true, it was a bad death," she mused.

"Very bad," the Sheriff agreed.

"The spirit is going to require some talking to…"

"Besides, the family asked special for you," he said.

No doubt because they didn't have any other choice, I thought. That morning, I'd run into Chinky Malloy, the assistant mortician at the Paradise, so I happened to know that Clinton was at a mortician's conference in the city and wouldn't be back for several days. But I didn't say a word.

23

(David Mura, 1952—)
大卫·村

作者简介

  大卫·村（David Mura, 1952— ），三世美国日裔著名诗人、作家。他出生于伊利诺伊州大湖区（Great Lakes, Illinois）。1970年，他进入艾奥瓦州的格林奈尔学院（Grinnell College, Iowa），主修政治学和英语；他于1974年毕业，获得学士学位。村在明尼苏达大学开始了自己英语专业的研究生阶段学习，但没有完成学业。1984年，他获得了美国/日本创意艺术家奖学金，在日本待了一年。1991年，他终于获得了佛蒙特学院的艺术硕士学位。大卫·村的创作生涯始于1980年代中期，尽管没有经历过拘留营的痛苦往事，但是他的主要作品仍然是以日裔的拘留营经历为题材。他目前已经出版了两本回忆录：《变成日本人：三世回忆录》(Turning Japanese: Memoirs of a Sansei, 1991) 和《身体与记忆相会之处》(Where the Body Meets Memory: An Odyssey of Race, Sexuality and Identity, 1995)，四部诗集：《迷路之后》(After We Lost Our Way, 1989)、《欲望的颜色》(The Colors of Desire, 1995)、《燃烧的天使》(Angels for the Burning: Poems, 2004) 和《最后的咒语》(The Last Incantations, 2014) 以及一部小说《日本帝国的著名自杀案》(Famous Suicides of the Japanese Empire, 2008)。村也从事其他形式的艺术，如表演、戏剧和电影等。此外，他还撰写了大量的文章和散文。

  村的诗歌关注自己的家族史、美国日裔社区历史以及个人身份。他总是将日裔个体、身份与他所处时代的历史背景，如第二次世界大战中美国日裔被监禁相联系。《欲望的颜色》中的诗歌在关注这些主题的同时，也仔细地审视了日裔第二次世界大战前的生活。下文节选部分为诗集的同名诗歌《欲望的颜色》，作者通过叙述美国社会对有色人种的限制，批判了美国的种族歧视政策。

作品选读

The Colors of Desire

1 *Photograph of a Lynching (circa 1930)*
These men? In their dented felt hats,
in the way their fingers tug their suspenders or vests,
with faces a bit puffy or too lean, eyes narrow and close together,
they seem too like our image of the South,
the Thirties. Of course they are white;
who then could create this cardboard figure, face
flat and grey, eyes oversized, bulging like
an ancient totem this gang has dug up? At the far right,
in a small browed cap, a boy of twelve smiles,
as if responding to what's most familiar here:
the camera's click. And though directly above them,
a branch ropes the dead negro in the air,
the men too focus their blank beam
on the unseen eye. Which is, at this moment, us.

Or, more precisely, me. Who cannot but recall
how my father, as a teenager, clutched his weekend pass,
passed through the rifle towers and gates
of the Jerome, Arkansas, camp, and, in 1942,
stepped on a bus to find white riders
motioning, "Sit here, son," and, in the rows beyond,
a half dozen black faces, waving him back,
"Us colored folks got to stick together."
How did he know where to sit? And how is it,
thirty-five years later, I found myself sitting
in a dark theater, watching *Behind the Green Door*

with a dozen anonymous men? On the screen
a woman sprawls on a table, stripped, the same one
on the Ivory Snow soap box, a baby on her shoulder,
smiling her blond, practically pure white smile.
Now, after being prepared and serviced slowly
by a handful of women, as one of them
kneels, buries her face in her crotch,
she is ready: And now he walks in—

Lean, naked, black, streaks of white paint on his chest
and face, a necklace of teeth, it's almost comical,
this fake garb of the jungle, Africa and All-America,
black and blond, almost a joke but for the surge
of what these lynchers urged as the ultimate crime
against nature: the black man kneeling to this kidnapped
body, slipping himself in, the screen showing it all, down
to her head shaking in a seizure, the final scream
before he lifts himself off her quivering body...

I left that theater, bolted from a dream into a dream.
I stared at the cars whizzing by, watched the light change,
red, yellow, green, and the haze in my head from the hash,
and the haze in my head from the image, melded together, reverberating.
I don't know what I did afterwards. Only, night after night,
I will see those bodies, black and white (and where am I,
the missing third?), like a talisman, a rageful, unrelenting release.

2 *1957*

Cut to Chicago, June. A boy of six.
Next year my hero will be Mickey Mantle,
but this noon, as father eases the Bel-Air past Wilson,
with cowboy hat black, cocked at an angle,
my skin dark from the sun, I'm Paladin,
and my six-guns point at cars whizzing past,

blast after blast ricocheting the glass.
Like all boys in such moments, my face
attempts a look of what—toughness? bravado? ease?—
until, impatient, my father's arm wails
across the seat, and I sit back, silent at last.

Later, as we step from IGA with our sacks,
a man in a serge suit—stained with ink?—
steps forward, shouts, "Hey, you a Jap?
You from Tokyo? You a Jap? A Chink?"
I stop, look up, I don't know him,
my arm yanks forward, and suddenly,
the sidewalk's rolling, buckling, like lava melting,
and I know father will explode,
shouts, fists, I know his temper.
And then,
I'm in that dream where nothing happens—
The ignition grinds, the man's face presses
the windshield, and father stares ahead,
fingers rigid on the wheel...

That night in my bedroom, moths,
like fingertips, peck the screen;
from the living room, the muffled t.v.
As I imagine Shane stepping into the dusty street,
in the next bed, my younger brother starts
to taunt—*you can't hurt me, you can't hurt me...*
Who can explain where this chant began?
Or why, when father throws the door open,
shouts stalking chaos erupted in his house,
he swoops on his son with the same swift motion
that the son, like an animal, like a scared and angry little boy,
fell on his brother, beating him in the dark?

3 Miss June 1964

I'm twelve, home from school
with a slight fever. I slide back the door
of my parents' closet—my mother's out shopping—
rummage among pumps, flats, lined in a rack,
unzip the garment bags, one by one.
It slides like a sigh from the folded sweaters.
I flip through ads for cologne, L.P.'s, a man
in a trench coat, lugging a panda-sized Fleischman's fifth.
Somewhere past the photo of Schweitzer
in his pith helmet, and the cartoon nude man
perched as a gargoyle, I spill the photo
millions of men, white, black, yellow, have seen,
though the body before me is white, eighteen:
Her breasts are enormous, almost
frightening
—the areolas seem large as my fist.
As the three glossy pages sprawl before me,
I start to touch myself, and there is
some terror, my mother will come home,
some delight I've never felt before,
and I do not cry out, I make no sound...

How did I know that photo was there?
Or mother know I knew?
Two nights later, at her request,
father lectures me on burning out too early.
Beneath the cone of light at the kitchen table,
we're caught, like the shiest of lovers.
He points at the booklet from the AMA
—he writes their P.R.—"Read it," he says,
"and, if you have any questions…"
Thirty years later, these questions remain.
And his answers, too, are still the same:

Really, David, it was just a magazine.
And the camps, my father's lost nursery,
the way he chased me round the yard in L.A.,
even the two by four he swung—why connect them
with years you wandered those theaters?
Is nothing in your life your own volition?
The past isn't just a box full of horrors.
What of those mornings in the surf
near Venice, all of us casting line after line,
arcing over breakers all the way from Japan,
or plopping down beside my mother,
a plateful of mochi, *pulling it like taffy*
with our teeth, shoyu *dribbling*
down our chins. Think of it, David.
There were days like that. We were happy....

4

Who hears the rain churning the forest to mud,
or the unraveling rope snap, the negro
plummet to rest at last? And what flooded my father's eyes
in the Little Rock theater, sitting beneath the balcony
in that third year of war? Where is 1944,
its snows sweeping down Heart Mountain,
to vanish on my mother's black bobbing head,
as she scurries towards the cramped cracked barracks
where her mother's throat coughs through the night,
and her father sits beside her on the bed?
The dim bulb flickers as my mother enters.
Her face is flushed, her cheeks cold. She
bows, unwraps her scarf, pours the steaming
kettle in the tea pot; offers her mother a sip.
And none of them knows she will never
talk of this moment, that, years later,
I will have to imagine it, again and again,

just as I have tried to imagine the lives
of all those who have entered these lines...

Tonight snow drifts below my window,
and lamps puff ghostly aureoles
over walks and lawns. Father, mother,
I married a woman not of my color.
What is it I want to escape?
These nights in our bed, my head
on her belly, I can hear these thumps,
and later, when she falls asleep,
I stand in our daughter's room,
so bare yet but for a simple wooden crib
(on the bulletin board I've pinned the sonogram
with black and white swirls like a galaxy
spinning about the fetal body),
and something plummets inside me,
out of proportion to the time
I've been portioned on this earth.
And if what is granted erases nothing,
if history remains, untouched, implacable,
as darkness flows up our hemisphere,
her hollow still moves moonward,
small hill on the horizon, swelling,
floating with child, white, yellow,
who knows, who can tell her,

oh why must it matter?

24

(Cynthia Kadohata, 1956—)
辛西娅·角畑

作者简介

辛西娅·角畑（Cynthia Kadohata, 1956— ）出生于芝加哥，父母均是美国日裔。其父母为了谋生，曾辗转于美国多地，童年漂泊的生活成为她日后进行文学创作的灵感来源。角畑在南加州大学（University of Southern California）完成自己的本科学业，后来在匹兹堡大学（University of Pittsburgh）和哥伦比亚大学（Columbia University）修读研究生学位。她是一个多产的作家，目前已出版了11部小说、一本插画图书，以及很多零散发表在杂志上的短篇故事。以2000年为界，角畑的小说创作可以分为两个阶段。第一阶段的小说主要是面向成人读者，共有三部：《漂浮的世界》（*The Floating World*, 1989）、《在爱之谷的中心》（*In the Heart of the Valley of Love*, 1992）、《玻璃山》（*The Glass Mountains*, 1995）；2000年之后，角畑的创作开始转向儿童文学，专为9—14岁的青少年写作文学作品。这期间她发表了8部小说，包括《亮晶晶》（*Kira-Kira*, 2004）、《野草花》（*Weed Flower*, 2006）、《侦探犬克拉克》（*Cracker! The Best Dog in Vietnam*, 2007）、《一百万度灰》（*A Million Shades of Gray*, 2010）、《明天会有好运气》（*The Thing about Luck*, 2013）、《半个世界之外》（*Half a World Away*, 2014）、《阻截》（*Checked*, 2018）以及《何处为家》（*A Place to Belong*, 2019）等。角畑小说的主题通常是爱、勇气、忠诚、责任、成长等，通过技巧性的陈述，让读者感受到温暖和力量，以充满希望的态度面对生活。

《何处为家》是角畑为中学生读者写的一部小说，主题是希望与归属感以及对日本文化的理解。故事讲述的是出生在美国的日裔女孩花子（Hanako）的故事。

日本偷袭珍珠港后，花子一家人和其他日本人一起被关押在美国拘留营中。战争结束后，他们一家回到了日本，以为和花子的祖父母住在一起生活会好一些。但是日本的生活更加艰难：饥饿一直是他们面临的最大威胁，贫困的家庭看不到改善状况的希望。最后父亲决定把花子和弟弟送回美国和亲戚住在一起。虽然花子一开始很不情愿，但她意识到父亲已经做出了他认为最好的决定。节选部分为小说的第六章，叙述花子一家刚到拘留营的状况，以及花子回忆日裔被美国政府强制迁移之前，她帮助父亲经营餐馆。

作品选读

A Place to Belong

Chapter Six

As her eyes adjusted, Hanako could see that the barrack was long and plain and empty. A soldier was already moving through the room throwing out bags of what he called *katapan* to eat, and everybody scrambled madly. Hanako pounced on some bags, grabbing them up greedily. She wasn't even sure what *katapan* was! She felt like an animal! Then she calmly handed all the bags to Akira, except for one each that she gave to Papa and Mama. Then Akira handed her a bag. "Here," he said. "I'll trade you for a piece of gum." So she traded.

Katapan turned out to be crackers. The hardest crackers in history, maybe. Biting them was like a battle between her teeth and the crackers, but then Mama told her to suck on one until it softened.

The crackers didn't have much taste, but they settled nicely in Hanako's stomach, taking away her hunger. After they finished eating, Mama told them to go to sleep since there was nothing else to do. There were hard platforms to sleep on. She and Akira lay down in their coats like their mother told them to, and they tried to sleep. Hanako was chilly and knew her brother would be too, so she wrapped her arms around him.

She was wide awake. In the dark barrack she could vividly picture their restaurant, the way she liked to do when she couldn't sleep. It was called the Weatherford Chinese & American Café. The restaurant had been their whole life, especially for Papa, but for

Hanako as well once she got old enough to work, which was the day she turned six. During their last summer of freedom before the war, she would get up with Papa at four thirty a.m. to eat breakfast and go to work, even though she was only seven. In many Nikkei families, you began working as soon as you could, babysitting or cooking rice or cleaning floors. Or filling salt shakers. Wiping counters. When Hanako and her father arrived at the restaurant each morning, Hanako would heat up the grill and turn on the steam table in the kitchen while Papa made coffee. Then Papa would make the batter for the pancakes and waffles. Breakfast was purely American, though most of their customers were Nikkei. But first-generation Japanese Americans—called Nisei—had embraced America completely. They were more American than a lot of Americans. Hanako would take out ten flats of thirty eggs—one by one, so as not to break any—and place them near the grill. Then she would bring other foods—like hash brown potatoes, bacon, and sausage—out of the refrigerator and place it all near the grill as well, ready to be cooked when an order was placed. Throughout the breakfast rush, she would make sure whatever food was needed was in the kitchen for the cooks.

After breakfast ended, Papa would start getting the food ready for lunch. He always had a daily lunch special and a daily soup. Around ten a.m. he would make six pies for the day. Dessert choices were the pie of the day, ice cream, or Jell-O. The pies for the week were apple, lemon meringue, pear, pineapple, cherry, and egg custard—for Tuesdays through Sundays. They were closed on Mondays. While Papa made the pies, Hanako would read a book in the office with Sadie.

Then during the lunch rush, Hanako again made sure the right foods were always in the kitchen for the cooks. They would yell out at her what was needed from the refrigerator. When lunch ended, she would blanch whole almonds by boiling them just until their skins puffed up. Then she drained the almonds onto a large, flat cookie sheet. After that she would squeeze the almonds from the fat ends, so that the nuts would pop out of the skins. The difficult part was to split the almonds in half. Hanako had to use a knife to split each almond on the seam. She would make seventy cookies with the almonds three times a week, plus one large cookie for herself and Akira to share. Toward the end she would be tired of making the cookies and didn't pay good attention to the baking. Sometimes the last batch was overcooked, and Papa would scold her. He used to say that being a perfectionist was one of life's most important secrets.

The restaurant closed at nine p.m., but Mama would come pick Hanako up at eight o'clock and take her home.

At night Papa would continue working until everything was clean and ready for tomorrow. Hanako wasn't sure what time he got home, because she would be asleep with Sadie next to her head on the pillow. Sometimes on top of her head, actually.

Mama worked too, when Akira was sleeping. She would save old grease and mix it with lye and water to make dishwashing soap. So nothing was wasted. Even the ugliest pan of grease was special.

It was all very hard work, but Hanako loved it because her father's ambition rubbed off on her. He was born ambitious to be a great cook, way back in another time, way back in America, which was now across the ocean. It was all in his mind now, though, wanting to cook.

Papa said all of that life—every single thing—was done and over with Kaput. He especially blamed President Roosevelt for their whole situation, as well as the ACLU, who mostly didn't stick up for them. Papa had explained it all to Hanako. The ACLU was a bunch of lawyers who'd formed an organization to defend people's civil rights and stand up for the Constitution. Supposedly, they had a lot of integrity. But their leadership voted not to challenge Roosevelt's order allowing the government to "exclude" people—namely, Nikkei—from "military areas"—namely, the West Coast, where most of the Nikkei lived. That had really surprised Papa, because he had always believed that there were special people—people born special, just like he was born to cook. He thought those people became president. He thought those people ran the ACLU. But in the end they weren't so special. "They're just like you and me," he had told Hanako. "Except they're lawyers."

And so here she was, in Japan, where her father could not see a future, but where he thought they could survive. If she were smarter, she would be able to understand time the way he did. There was a part of her that sometimes couldn't quite comprehend how things could just be gone. She had to tell herself over and over that her old life would not return. A part of her did not believe it the way her father did.

She felt a rush of love for Papa, and for her whole family, lying there near her, on these hard platforms in a new and strange land. She felt that anger that made her face hot and made her squeeze her hands into fists. She had no future! All she had was her trust in her parents. Then her anger started to subside. Even though Papa said he could not see the future yet, Hanako believed that he would see it again, and soon. Maybe more than wanting to cook, he was born wanting to see the future. He said that was why he and Mama got along. She took care of what was going on *now*, and he took care of the future. That way, Hanako and Akira were covered, in the present and hopefully forever.

25

(Ruth L. Ozeki, 1956—)
露丝·尾关

作者简介

露丝·尾关（Ruth L. Ozeki, 1956—）是当代美国文坛最受关注的日裔作家之一，同时也是一位著名的电影制片人。她出生于美国康涅狄格州的纽黑文（New Haven, Connecticut），是一位美日混血儿，父亲是美国的一位语言学家和研究玛雅文化的人类学家，母亲是日本人。在史密斯学院（Smith College）完成自己的本科学业之后，尾关到日本的奈良大学学习日本古典文学，并广泛地涉猎了日本传统文化、技艺等。尾关是一名禅宗信徒，禅宗思想对她本人影响很大，因而尾关作品中很多地方都可以看到禅宗思想的痕迹。回到美国后，尾关曾经拍摄过纪录片和电影，后来转为文学创作。1998年，她出版了自己的处女作《食肉之年》(*My Year of Meat*)，这本书获得极大成功，获得了《纽约时报》年度好书的称号，桐山环太平洋图书奖（Kiriyama Prize）以及艾莫斯/巴尼斯和诺布尔美国图书奖（Imus/Barnes & Noble American Book Award）。2003年，尾关出版了第二部小说《天下苍生》(*All over Creation*)，获得了该年度的美国图书奖。2013年，尾关又出版了第三部作品《不存在的女孩》(*A Tale for the Time Being*)，同样受到评论界欢迎，入围该年度的曼布克奖（Man Booker Prize），夺得《纽约时报书评》编辑选择和独立书商图书奖，2014年又获得加拿大日本文学奖。

尾关的作品通常是以女性的视角关注自然与科学，探讨人类历史、文化身份以及政治问题，揭示了当代社会中存在的危机以及生态问题。《天下苍生》这部小说审视了企业生活、全球化、政治抵抗、青年文化和"婴儿潮"一代老龄化等主题。小说讲述了一个关于转基因工程植物（即土豆）究竟是破坏环境，还是把世界从饥荒中拯救出来的故事。小说主人公富勒由美（Yumi Fuller）是一个美国日裔，她的父亲是艾奥瓦州的一名马铃薯种植者。时隔25多年后，由美回到家中照顾父母，陷入了围绕转基因食品日益激烈的争议。她被卷入了一场新的、意想不到的困境：由美生活的农业社区遭到了与激进组织"抵抗种子"（Seeds of Resistance）作战的农业企业势力的入侵。小说也颂扬了种子、根和所有生长事物的美丽。节选部分为《天下苍生》的第二章，由美时隔多年之后返回故乡与旧友重聚。

作品选读

All over Creation

Reunion
(Excerpt)

After all these years, Cass couldn't get the phrase out of her head. She stood by the window in the arrivals lounge with her forehead pressed to the glass. The reflection of the red and green Christmas lights that decorated the lounge appeared to be floating against the dark tarmac outside. It was cold, and snow conditions east of the Cascades had delayed the plane. She had driven up from Liberty Falls just after one o'clock, and now it was late afternoon, and the prairie wind was whipping the snow around the tarmac, just mocking the plows.

She went back to the bar to have a cigarette. Not that she was supposed to be smoking. After the operation she'd more or less quit—she didn't smoke at home at all anymore, didn't even keep cigarettes around—but when she'd gotten in the car that morning, she knew she would smoke again for old time's sake, and as soon as she'd passed the Liberty Falls town-limits sign, she pulled into a 7-Eleven and bought a pack of Old Gold Filters. Will would kill her if he found out, but the thought of seeing Yummy made her crave it again. She smoked with the car window open. Her fingers were like ice on the wheel. If Will asked, she could blame the smell on Yummy.

She ordered another coffee, bypassed the sugar, and dumped in two packets of Nutrasweet. She was trying to be healthy, after all these years.

At four she phoned Will on the cell phone.

At five she had a hot dog and a Coors and another cigarette.

Finally, just after six, she heard the announcement for the Seattle flight. A small crowd had gathered by the gate. They were the same bored people she'd seen waiting all day, but now, one by one, their faces lit up as a long-awaited loved one emerged from the plane. Cassie's face felt frozen. Not eager. Not lit. She wondered if Yummy would recognize her. She was certain she would have no trouble recognizing Yummy Fuller.

And she didn't. Yummy hadn't changed at all. No. She *had* changed. She was taller, and older, of course. Her skin had relaxed about the eyes and cheeks, but her face was burnished by the sun. The people around her—dull, soft-bodied, and white— seemed to squint when they caught sight of her, she was just that bright. She wore cropped pants and a long, loose coat made out of linen, outrageously tropical among the massing Polyfill parkas that eddied around her like lumpy clouds. She scanned the faces, and when her eyes came to rest on Cass, she frowned and cocked her head, combing the jet-black hair away from her forehead with her fingers.

"Cass?" she mouthed. "Is that you?"

Cass managed a nod, and she watched Yummy part the crowd with the ease of Moses. Then, before she knew it, they were standing face-to-face, and Cass found herself stepping back, the way you sometimes do when you walk out into a strong wind.

"Wow, Yummy said. "Cassie Unger."

"Hi," Cass said. Then she added, "It's Quinn now."

Yummy didn't seem to hear. "You grew."

"Yes. I guess. So did you."

"You're almost as tall as me."

"Not really." Cass tried not to slouch. "You're still taller."

"You've lost your baby fat." Yummy grinned and stepped back to appraise her. "Skinny, even."

Cass crossed her arms in front of her chest.

"Hey, no," Yummy said. "You look great. Just surprised me. Like a different person."

"Yes," Cass said. "I am."

"Hmmm…" Yummy said, drawing out the sound, as though unclear as to whether she agreed. "I guess we have changed, after all these years."

"Yes," Cass said. "After all these years."

Three children moved in a loose orbit around Yummy, like insects looking for a place to land. They were obviously attached to her, but they did not look much related.

"Are those your kids?" Cass asked.

"All three of 'em. Feels like a lot more. Do you have any?"

Cass shook her head.

"Well, you can have some of mine." She gestured impatiently to a skinny Asian boy with a baby on his hip, who ambled over, pushing an empty stroller. Yummy took the baby and gave the boy a shove toward Cass. "This is Phoenix. Phoenix, this is Cassie Unger. Sorry, Quinn. She lives next door to your *kupuna*."

It was a week before Christmas, and the boy was wearing a T-shirt and baggy shorts that came down to his knees, and his legs stuck out underneath like thin brown sticks. Scuffy sneakers. No socks. His bushy black hair stood up in bristles. Cass held out her hand to shake, but he drew his away and made a fist, leaving the thumb and pinkie standing. This he waggled at her.

"Howzit," he said. "You can call me Nix."

"He's fourteen," Yummy explained, setting the squirming baby down on his bottom, on the floor. "He's in the process of rejecting everything his mother ever gave him. Including his name."

"Oh, Yummy, that's such crap," Phoenix said.

"See what I mean?" Yummy smiled. She lowered her voice and spoke in a stage whisper. "Phoenix, remember what I told you. This is Idaho. Call me Mommy, and stop swearing or the townsfolk will lynch you." Phoenix rolled his eyes while Yummy grabbed another child, a fair-haired girl with sea blue eyes. "This one's Ocean. She's six and a half."

"Ocean has a nickname, too," Phoenix offered.

"Shuddup!" yelled Ocean.

"It's Puddle," Phoenix said with an evil smile.

"It is NOT!"

"And this is Poo," Phoenix offered smoothly, ducking Ocean's fist and capturing the escaping baby by the back of his suspenders. "He's not doing the walking thing yet." The baby sat on the floor and looked up at Cass, flapping his arms a little. His skin was the color of milk chocolate. Curls sprang from his head, each a soft and perfect vortex.

"What's his real name?" Cass asked.

"Just Poo. Mommy was striking out with the names, so she kind of just gave up." He picked the baby up and offered him to Cass. "Here. Wanna hold him?"

Cass took the baby in her arms. He was heavy and warm.

"That's not true, Phoenix," Yummy said. She turned to Cass. "His name is Barnabas, but he has to grow into it. For now Poo suits him just fine."

"Hello, Poo," Cass said. His eyes were liquid black. He gurgled and patted her cheek.

They collected their suitcases, and Cass waited while they opened them and dug out warm clothes; then she led them out to the parking lot. She felt like a ringmaster at a carnival parade. Their bags filled the back of the Suburban.

"It's freezing," Phoenix said, teeth chattering.

"It'll warm up once we get going," Cass told him.

Ocean climbed into the backseat next to her brother. "Yuuuck! This car stinks."

Yummy turned around. "Ocean, shut up."

"But it does!"

"Ocean—" There was a warning in Yummy's voice now.

The little girl subsided. "It smells like *cigarettes*," she whispered to Phoenix.

"So what?"

"I bet the lady smokes *cigarettes*."

"Why don't you ask her?"

Ocean leaned forward. "Excuse me," she said, tapping Cass on the shoulder. Cass glanced into the rearview as she put the car into reverse and backed out of the space.

"Do you smoke *cigarettes*?"

"Sometimes," she answered the child in the mirror. "Not often."

Ocean's face grew severe. "You shouldn't smoke cigarettes," she said. "*Ever*."

"I know."

"But do you know why you shouldn't?"

vegetative activity. But here…"

"It's quiet, all right. Not much happens in winter. Aside from the storms."

26

(Velina Hasu Houston, 1957—)
韦丽娜·芳须·休斯敦

作者简介

韦丽娜·芳须·休斯敦（Velina Hasu Houston, 1957—）拥有日本、美国非裔和美国原住民血统。休斯敦出生在东京，母亲是日本人，父亲是一名美国占领军士兵。1959年，休斯敦随父母移居美国，先是住在纽约，然后定居在堪萨斯州。1969年，父亲去世后，她一直和母亲住在一起。1979年，休斯敦在堪萨斯州立大学（Kansas State University）获得新闻、大众传播和戏剧专业的学士学位，之后她继续学习戏剧艺术和剧本创作，并于1981年在加州大学洛杉矶分校（UCLA）获得文学硕士学位。她的作品《早晨醒来》（*Morning Has Broken*, 1981）是她在加州大学洛杉矶分校学习时创作的作品，发表在她本人编辑的《生活的政治：四部美国亚裔女性戏剧》（*The Politics of Life: Four Plays by Asian American Women*, 1993）。休斯敦其他主要戏剧还有《茶》（*Tea*, 1993）、《松山镜》（*The Matsuyama Mirror*, 1996）、《真心》（*Kokoro*, 1997）、《草裙舞之心》（*Hula Heart*, 1999）等。同时，休斯敦还有一些未发表的戏剧：《没人像我们一样》（*Nobody Like Us*, 1979）、《饥渴》（*Thirst*, 1981）、《美国梦》（*American Dreams*, 1983）、《美亚混血女孩》（*Amerasian Girls*, 1983）、《信天翁》（*Albatross*, 1988）、《圣诞蛋糕》（*Christmas Cake*, 1990）、《华道》（*Ikebana*, 1999）、《等待正志》（*Waiting for Tadashi*, 1999）等作品。休斯敦的戏剧成就为她赢得了许多著名奖项，包括1982年的"罗兰·汉斯贝利剧本写作奖"（Lorraine Hansberry Playwriting Award）、1984年的"《洛杉矶周报》戏剧评论家奖"（*LA Weekly* Drama Critics Award）、1991年的"《洛杉矶时报》和戏剧评论家选择奖"（Critics' Choice

Awards from the *Los Angeles Times* and Drama Logue）以及1996年"波奥克拉奖"（Po'Okela Award）等奖项。

《清晨醒来》虽然不完全是休斯敦的自传，但是反映了她的家庭历史和她自己的跨种族背景，以及几个不变的主题：妇女、种族关系、性别问题和国家边界。这部戏剧本质上是一部日本戏剧，它讲述了日本从战前传统父权家庭结构向战后更加民主家庭关系的转变，以及这种转变对家庭性别角色的影响。这部剧也是跨国界、跨种族的，因为它涉及日本和美国，以及美国占领军中的一名美国非洲裔士兵。下文节选部分为本剧的第二场。日本女孩静子（Setsuko）、富美子（Fumiko）与美国非裔士兵克里德（Creed）相遇在神户街头。

作品选读

Morning Has Broken

Asa Ga Kimashita

Scene Two

(Lights fade in downstage right accompanied by the sounds of a city. Kobe, Japan. Enter SETSUKO. She wears a beautiful kimono and walks with a slow, graceful gait. She carries an armful of books, a furoshiki full of dressmaking paraphernalia, and a packet of patterns in her hand. Her cousin FUMIKO dressed in American clothes, walks briskly a step ahead of her. FUMIKO is willful; she knows she is lovely. She wears an American ensemble including hat and gloves. Offstage, a horn beeps and a U.S. Army helmet rolls onstage in front of the women. They stop abruptly and look in the direction from which it came. Enter CREED, a handsome and regal African American with a gentle smile. FUMIKO's eyes grow wide at the sight of CREED. But CREED sees only Setsuko, who is immediately shy and deferential. SETSUKO drops down on her knees and bows, not looking up at him. FUMIKO screams in shock and faints. SETSUKO is afraid to get up and help her. CREED takes out a handkerchief and pats FUMIKO's brow.)

SETSUKO: Please forgive our clumsiness, honorable American.
CREED: You didn't do anything wrong. Is she going to be okay?

SETSUKO *(still not looking up)*: She has never seen ... one of you. *(a beat)* I have never seen one of you either. *(looks and quickly looks away)*

CREED: A colored man, you mean.

SETSUKO: Yes. We apologize for our rudeness.

CREED: Maybe I was driving too fast—or paying attention to something other than my driving. Miss? Please stand up or look up or something.

SETSUKO *(barely daring to look up)*: Forgive me.

CREED: Will you please stop apologizing? There's so much charm in this country that I just might choke on it. Gee, she's really out cold.

SETSUKO *(represses a giggle, as does CREED)*: It is funny to see her in this state. She is usually so ... perfect.

(FUMIKO *starts to revive. She sees* CREED *and screams again.* SETSUKO *muffles it with her hand.* FUMIKO *sits up and stares at* CREED.)

FUMIKO: What are you?

CREED *(a gentle smile)*: A human being.

FUMIKO: I am sorry. I've never seen one quite like you. What do they call you?

CREED: Negro, colored, other things I don't want to repeat in front of ladies. But I call myself a colored man because my mama was red and my papa was brown.

FUMIKO: Are there many of you ... colored skins?

CREED: Brown, yellow, dark brown. You name it. We got it.

(SETSUKO *retrieves the helmet, bows, and hands it to* CREED.)

CREED: Thank you. Would you ladies like a ride in my jeep?

FUMIKO *(points toward audience)*: Look, Setchan! That mama-san is already staring at us! Like we just dropped off the moon or something! *(waves at the offstage mama-san, speaks to mamasan)* "... bless America!" "Hail to the emperor!"

SETSUKO: Fumiko-san, enough. A crowd is gathering.

FUMIKO *(to CREED)*: We would love to take that ride. What is your name?

CREED: Creed Banks.

SETSUKO: A pleasure to make your acquaintance, sir.

FUMIKO: Oh stop with the bowing, cousin! *(to* CREED*)* She is from the provinces. She does not know that you people do not bow. (CREED *helps her stand and* SETSUKO *dusts dirt from her dress. He bows to* SETSUKO.)

CREED: Very pleased to make your acquaintance. *(quickly, to* FUMIKO *without a bow)* And yours, too. *(smiles and bows formally)*

(FUMIKO stares at CREED again in renewed awe, as CREED picks up SETSUKO's belongings and gestures for them to go ahead of him toward the offstage jeep. She breaks out in a grin, having decided that she likes him.)
FUMIKO: Imagine that! A brown American!
(Lights crossfade to Scene Three.)

27

(Kyoko Mori, 1957—)
森京子

作者简介

　　森京子（Kyoko Mori, 1957—）出生在日本神户，之后前往美国洛克福德学院（Rockford College）学习，并于1979年获得学士学位。1981年，她在密尔沃基的威斯康星大学（University of Wisconsin）获得硕士学位，1984年获得博士学位。她的博士论文由一组故事组成，这也成为她第一部小说《静子的女儿》（*Shizuko's Daughter*, 1993）的基础。她的第二部小说《一只鸟》（*One Bird*）于1995年出版，2000年她又出版了小说《石场，真箭》（*Stone Field, True Arrow*）。森京子的非小说作品包括《水之梦》（*The Dream of Water*, 1995）以及《礼貌的谎言：一个文化间隙中的女人》（*Polite Lies: On Being a Woman Caught between Cultures*, 1998），记录了1990年她休假期间在日本旅行期间发生的事件，并以叙述者的口吻讲述了她的成长经历。同时她还出版了诗集《脱落》（*Fall Out*, 1994）。

　　森京子的小说《静子的女儿》是写给年轻读者的，被《纽约时报》评为最佳儿童读物。故事情节与森京子本人的生活非常相似。故事的女主人公友纪（Yuki）在成长过程中经历了非常困难甚至是创伤性的事件，如母亲自杀死亡和她受到父亲和继母虐待等。友纪在失去母亲的痛苦中长大，她努力在父权制的世界里定义自己的身份。这部小说探索了一个生活在日本的青春期少女反抗父亲强加给她的严格纪律和日本文化的故事。由于种种原因，友纪在整个故事中经常感到孤独，其中一个重要原因是她拒绝与那些逆来顺受地接受生活现状的人为伍。节选部分为小说的第二章，友纪的母亲自杀身亡，她与姨妈一起整理母亲的遗物。

作品选读

Shizuko's Daughter

2

The Wake

(*March 1969*)

(Excerpt)

  The men were rearranging the living room for the wake. Upstairs, her aunt Aya, just arrived on the afternoon southbound train from Tokyo, began to put the clothes into wooden storage boxes for the attic. Yuki took down her mother's blue housecoat from the bathroom door and brought it to her aunt. A whole day had passed since her mother's death. Her father had not touched a single thing that had belonged to her mother, as though he thought of death as contagious.

  Aya took the housecoat from Yuki and put it away. "You can wear some of these when you grow up," she said, her hand sweeping over the clothes inside the box.

  Yuki sat down and watched as her aunt went back to the open closet. It was already half empty. Aya continued to take the remaining blouses and dresses off the hangers, fold them, and lay them inside the boxes. Off the hangers, the clothes suddenly collapsed and hung limp from Aya's hands. Yuki breathed in the faint smell of sawdust from the boxes. The soft silks and cottons Aya was putting away still smelled of her mother. They were mostly in shades of green and blue. Soon, the closet was empty and the boxes were full. Her aunt poured out a handful of mothballs into each box and closed the lid on her mother's colors. Yuki imagined the smell of mothballs and dust filtering through them in the dark.

  Aya shut the closet door and went to the bureau. From the top drawers, she pulled out a handful of silk scarves and jewelry and turned back to Yuki. "You've been so good," she said. "At your age, it must be so difficult."

  Yuki looked away and at the photograph on the wall. On its glass frame the late-afternoon sun cast weak shadows of the fir trees outside, their branches swaying now and then in the breeze. It was like a double exposure: the moving branches outside superimposed on the still photograph of her family three or four years ago. In the photograph her mother stood between Yuki and her father, one hand on his arm and the other on Yuki's shoulder.

"Nobody would think you were only twelve," Aya said. "The way you've been acting, with such composure." She began to fold the scarves and stack them up on a pile of small articles to be distributed among friends and relatives as keepsakes. "You didn't even cry once."

Yuki was sick of such remarks: "You've been so good," "You're only twelve," "So brave." It seemed as though no one had said anything else to her since late yesterday afternoon, when, coming home from her piano lesson, she had found her mother unconscious on the kitchen floor.

She had dropped her books, turned off the gas, and called her father at work. He had told her not to call an ambulance and create a commotion—he would fetch a doctor himself and come home immediately. While she waited for them, Yuki opened the windows to let out the gas. Then she sat down and touched her mother's forehead. It felt surprisingly cool. The air from the windows might be too cold, she thought. She went and lowered the windows. Her mother was no longer breathing, and Yuki was not sure exactly when her breath had stopped. Now, a day later, the smell of gas seemed to cling to Yuki's clothes, her hair. She washed her hair over and over to get it out, but it lingered.

After the doctor had said that there was no hope, Yuki walked into the den and found the white cotton and maroon trimmings cut out for her new skirt and laid out on the sewing board. The triangular pieces, with silver tacks scattered over them, looked like the remnants of a shipwreck. And Yuki thought: When did you decide to do it? Just this morning you were trying to sew.

Even then, she didn't cry. She picked up her mother's address book from the desk and went to the hallway to phone her relatives and friends, absentmindedly staring at her mother's handwriting, while her father was in the kitchen with the two policemen who had been called by the doctor.

The sound of jangling metal made Yuki look up. Her aunt was now going through the jewelry and cosmetics left in the other drawers. They went in two piles, to be saved or discarded. Most of the jewelry would be saved, except for bracelets whose clasps no longer fastened, odd earrings that did not match, all the small broken things her mother had kept. The cosmetics would be discarded. As Aya swept a handful of lipstick and eye shadow off the pile into the wastebasket, one roll of lipstick slipped through her fingers and fell on the floor. The cap came off and the lipstick rolled to the edge of the carpet.

"Your poor mother," Aya said. She turned aside and pressed her fingers to her eyes.

Yuki picked up the lipstick. Its tip, cut at a sixty-degree angle, had scarcely been blunted. She put the cap back on and dropped the roll in the wastebasket, thinking of how the lipstick, too, smelled of her mother.

She had not been downstairs since the early afternoon. Yuki stood at the door of the living room, unable to go in. The room looked completely unfamiliar. She couldn't believe it was the same room where she and her mother had sat listening to music or drawing together, drinking tea after dinner and talking. Yuki stared silently at the makeshift altar, the coffin in the center, the white and yellow chrysanthemums drenched in the smoke from the incense sticks. White drapery was everywhere, covering the floor and the walls in large, billowy folds. Yuki tried to remember where each piece of furniture had been: the armchair where her mother had sat, the glass table on which they had put their cups of tea and plates of cake, the footstool where she had sat, always close enough to reach over and hand her mother a drawing to look at or a book to read, the piano she had played while her mother closed her eyes, listening. All these things had been moved out of the room or shoved behind the drapery.

28

(Julie Otsuka, 1962—)
朱莉·大塚

作者简介

朱莉·大塚（Julie Otsuka, 1962— ）出生在加州的帕洛阿尔托（Palo Alto, California）。她的父母都是日裔，父亲是航空工程师，母亲是实验室技术员。九岁时，她随家人搬到了加州的帕洛斯弗德斯（Palos Verdes, California）。高中毕业后，大塚进了耶鲁大学，并于1984年获得了文学学士学位。1999年毕业于哥伦比亚大学，获美术硕士学位。她的处女作《天皇神圣之时》（*When the Emperor Was Divine*, 2002）讲述了第二次世界大战期间美国日裔被非法拘留的故事。她的第二部小说《阁楼上的佛像》（*The Buddha in the Attic*, 2011）讲述了日本移民至美国的"照片新娘"的故事。大塚的小说获得过很多奖项，其中《天皇神圣之时》获得了美国亚裔文学奖（Asian American Literary Award）以及亚历克斯奖（Alex Award）；《阁楼上的佛像》入围过国家图书奖以及《洛杉矶时报》图书奖的决选名单，获得了笔会/福克纳小说奖以及美国历史小说朗格姆奖（Langum Prize for American Historical Fiction）。

大塚以描写美国日裔的历史小说而闻名。通过自己的作品，她试图唤起人们对第二次世界大战期间美国日裔困境的关注。《天皇神圣之时》是她第一部描写美国日裔拘留营经历的小说，描述了一个美国日裔家庭在第二次世界大战期间被关进拘留营的故事。小说描述了当时美国日裔的挣扎，以及他们在拘留期间和之后所面临的难以想象的恶劣生活条件。小说的前三章从母亲、11岁女儿和8岁儿子的视角来讲述；第四章通过"我们"的视角来讲述，试图将美国日裔作为一个整体来阐述这场斗争，而第五章从父亲的角度来讲述。节选部分为本书的《自白》一节，名为"自白"实为对美国政府的控诉。

作品选读

When the Emperor Was Divine

Confession

Everything you have heard is true. I was wearing my bathrobe, my slippers, the night your men took me away. At the station they asked me questions. *Talk to us*, they said. The room was small and bare. It had no windows. The lights were bright. They left them on for days. What more can I tell you? My feet were cold. I was tired. I was thirsty. I was scared. So I did what I had to do. I talked.

All right, I said. I admit it. I lied. You were right. You were always right. It was me. I did it. I poisoned your reservoirs. I sprinkled your food with insecticide. I sent my peas and potatoes to market full of arsenic. I planted sticks of dynamite alongside your railroads. I set your oil wells on fire. I scattered mines across the entrance to your harbors. I spied on your airfields. I spied on your naval yards. I spied on your neighbors. I spied on you—you get up at six, you like bacon and eggs, you love baseball, you take your coffee with cream, your favorite color is blue. I crept into your house while you were away and sullied your wife. *Wait, wait,* she said, *don't go.* I touched your daughters—they smiled in their sleep. I smothered your firstborn son—he did not struggle. I stole your last bag of sugar. I took a swig from your best bottle of brandy. I pulled out the nails from your white picket fence and sold them to the enemy to melt down and make into bullets. I gave that same enemy your defense maps for free. *The Boeing assembly plant is here*. The oil refinery, there. "X" marks the spot where they make the *camouflage nets*. I sent him aerial photographs of your major coastal cities. I radioed to his submarines the location of your troop ships. I leaned out my second-story window and signaled to his aviators with my red paper lantern. *Come on over*! I left my lights on during the blackout. I went out into the yard and tossed up a few flares just to make sure he knew where to find you. *Drop that bomb right here, right here where I'm standing!* I cut arrow-shaped swaths through my tomato fields to guide him to his next target. *Straight ahead to the air force base!* I told him all about you. *Tall and handsome. Big eyes. Long nose. Broad shoulders. Perfect teeth. Nice smile. Firm handshake. Solid family man. A joiner. Member of the Elks. The Kiwanis.*

The Rotary. The local Chamber of Commerce. Mows his lawn every Saturday and goes to church on Sundays. Pays his bills on time. Enjoys the occasional night out with the boys. Wife stays home and takes care of the kids. I revealed to him your worst secrets. *Short attention span. Doesn't always remember to take out the garbage. Sometimes talks with his mouth full.*

Who am I? You know who I am. Or you think you do. I'm your florist. I'm your grocer. I'm your porter. I'm your waiter. I'm the owner of the dry-goods store on the corner of Elm. I'm the shoeshine boy. I'm the judo teacher. I'm the Buddhist priest. I'm the Shinto priest. I'm the Right Reverend Yoshimoto. So *please to meet you*. I'm the general manager at Mitsubishi. I'm the dishwasher at the Golden Pagoda. I'm the janitor at the Claremont Hotel. I'm the laundryman. I'm the nurseryman. I'm the fisherman. I'm the ranch hand. I'm the farm hand. I'm the peach picker. I'm the pear picker. I'm the lettuce packer. I'm the oyster planter. I'm the cannery worker. I'm the chicken sexer. *And I know a healthy young rooster when I see one!* I'm the grinning fat man in the straw hat selling strawberries by the side of the road. I'm the president of the Cherry Blossom Society. I'm the secretary of the Haiku Association. I'm a card-carrying member of the Bonsai Club. *Such a delightful little people! Everything so small and pretty!* I'm the one you call Jap. I'm the one you call Nip. I'm the one you call Slits. I'm the one you call Slopes. I'm the one you call Yellowbelly. I'm the one you call Gook. I'm the one you don't see at all—we all look alike. I'm the one you see everywhere—we're taking over the neighborhood. I'm the one you look for under your bed every night before you go to sleep. *Just checking*, you say. I'm the one you dream of all night long—we're marching ten abreast down Main Street. I'm your nightmare—we're bivouacking tonight on your newly mowed front lawn. I'm your worst fear—you saw what we did in Manchuria, you remember Nanking, you can't get Pearl Harbor out of your mind.

I'm the slant-eyed sniper in the trees.

I'm the saboteur in the shrubs.

I'm the stranger at the gate.

I'm the traitor in your own backyard.

I'm your houseboy.

I'm your cook.

I'm your gardener.

And I've been living here, quietly, beside you, for years, just waiting for Tojo to flash me the high sign.

So go ahead and lock me up. Take my children. Take my wife. Freeze my assets. Seize my crops. Search my office. Ransack my house. Cancel my insurance. Auction off my business. Hand over my lease. Assign me a number. Inform me of my crime. *Too short, too dark, too ugly, too proud.* Put it down in writing—*is nervous in conversation, always laughs loudly at the wrong time, never laughs at all*—and I'll sign on the dotted line. *Is treacherous and cunning, is ruthless, is cruel.* And if they ask you someday what it was I most wanted to say, please tell them, if you would, it was this:

I'm sorry.

There. That's it. I've said it. Now can I go?

29

(Nina Revoyr, 1969—)
妮娜·雷伏娃

作者简介

妮娜·雷伏娃（Nina Revoyr, 1969— ）出生在日本，母亲是日本人，父亲是波兰裔美国人。她从耶鲁大学毕业后，到日本教了两年英语；之后，雷伏娃回到美国，在康奈尔大学获得了创意写作艺术硕士学位。1997 年她出版了自己的第一部小说《必要的饥饿》(*The Necessary Hunger*)。此后，她先后出版了《南国》(*Southland*, 2003)、《梦想的时代》(*The Age of Dreaming*, 2008)、《翼射手》(*Wingshooters*, 2011)、《失落的峡谷》(*Lost Canyon*, 2015) 以及《历史专业学生》(*A Student of History*, 2019) 等作品。

雷伏娃的作品主要植根于洛杉矶，既关乎地方，也关乎社区和居民。这些小说反映了一个复杂的、多种族的、不断演变的洛杉矶。种族、阶级、历史背景、政治议题都出现在她的小说中。在《翼射手》一书中，她将小说背景设置在 20 世纪 70 年代威斯康星州的农村地区，并将种族、阶级和家庭置于小城镇背景下。小说可以被视为主人公米歇尔·勒博（Michelle LeBeau）的成长传奇，故事发生的年代是后越南战争时期，社会动荡有增无减。还不到 10 岁的米歇尔·勒博被留在威斯康星州迪尔霍恩的蓝领小镇，和她的祖父母住在一起。这部小说从成年米歇尔的角度来讲述，对成年人的世界发表了深刻见解。

节选部分为小说的第一章，主要内容为米歇尔回忆居住在小镇上的祖父。

作品选读

Wingshooters

One
(Excerpt)

In my apartment in California there hangs a picture of my grandfather. He is one of twelve men dressed in off-white baseball uniforms and plain dark caps, all seated in front of a boy in a baggy black suit. The men sit cross-legged or rest on one knee; their bats lean together like logs on a camp fire, surrounded by their gloves. Behind them stand two large, boxy cars with a banner draped between them that reads, *Buick Ball Club, Deerhorn Wisconsin*. Although the picture is posed, there is something about the quality of the players' postures and smiles that makes it seem like they just collapsed there, giddy and tired, and someone happened to capture the moment. The uniforms have a softer look than what ballplayers wear today—the caps are rounder and more pliable, the pants and jerseys looser, the gloves amorphous and lumpy—but the men look more like men. My grandfather, sitting in the lower right-hand corner, smiles at the camera from out of his open, handsome face as if he knows he'll live forever. The license plate on one of the Buicks has tags from 1925, and if the date is accurate, then my grandfather, Charlie LeBeau, is nineteen. Because of the cap, the usual shock of slicked-back hair that falls over his eyes, making him look playful and roguish, is held still. But even so, he is beautiful, and knows it. Farther back in the picture, a young woman leans out the window of another car, resting her chin in her hand, and I imagine she is staring at Charlie. Everyone, for all of his life, always stared at Charlie.

My grandfather grew up in the country five miles outside of Deerhorn, and played ball in the evenings after long days out in the fields. His family grew corn and potatoes and barley, and raised cattle and pigs, until the Depression made it impossible to keep the farm running and they sold it and made the move into town. By that time, he was married to my grandmother, Helen Wilkes, whom he'd met at the one-room school just east of town. Charlie was never a student—he was two years behind his class when Helen sat down in front of him, and Helen a year ahead of hers, their respective talents and deficiencies erasing the gap of three years that divided them. He kept pulling on her pigtails as she tried to listen to the teacher, and she finally married him, she said, to make him stop. They married—eloped—when Charlie was twenty and Helen seventeen, so he already knew her when the picture of the baseball team was taken. It could be that the relaxed, self-satisfied grin on his face has something to do with her. It could also be that the girl in the car—whoever she is—knows this, and that's why she looks so sad.

  My grandfather never fought in a war. He was too young for the first great conflict in Europe, which took his father's brother, and too old for World War II. And he never held a position—say, sheriff or lawyer—that placed him above other men. No, Charlie LeBeau worked the same unforgiving, muscular jobs—at the meat processing plant, the car parts shop, the Stevenson shoe factory—that the other men did, but he always seemed larger than them, heroic. He was the best ballplayer in the region, a third baseman pursued by the White Sox, as his father had been twenty years before. But also like his father, he turned down the chance to enter the White Sox's minor league system because he wouldn't leave Central Wisconsin—and because he refused to play for the team that had recently thrown the World Series. He won the state skeet-shooting championship a half dozen times; I still have a letter, dated 1935, from the Thomason Gunworks Company, congratulating him on his perfect score in that year's contest and offering him a lifetime supply of free ammunition. He was simply, consistently the best shot in the state of Wisconsin, as he proved every fall by bagging more ducks, grouse, pheasants, and deer than his family could ever possibly eat. The gun case in my grandparents' dining room was his centerpiece, his shrine, filled with weapons of every size and capacity—some functional, some collectors' pieces purely for display, like the Springfield Rifle his uncle had used in the Great War. He also had three bows, regal, primal-looking things, and another case for his collection of fishing rods. Sometimes I would take out one of these rifles or bows just to hold it and feel the power it contained.

  But it wasn't his skill with weapons that set Charlie apart. It was the way that other people related to him. Men gathered around him at Jimmy's Coffee Shop or Earl's Gun Store or in his own house to hear him expound on everything from the proper training of hunting dogs to the town's new traffic light; women lowered their eyes and blushed when he was near. And he paid back and increased this devotion in a thousand small ways—by changing tires or plowing sidewalks for the widows in town; by welcoming unattached men into his house for Friday suppers; by taking young boys to the baseball fields to work on their games, or out into the deepest woods, to hunt.

30

(Brenda Shaughnessy, 1970—)
布伦达·肖内西

作者简介

布伦达·肖内西（Brenda Shaughnessy, 1970— ）是著名美国日裔诗人，出生于冲绳（Okinawa），在南加州长大。她在加州大学圣克鲁兹分校获得文学和女性研究学士学位，在哥伦比亚大学获得艺术硕士学位。她是罗格斯－纽瓦克大学（Rutgers-Newark）英语和艺术硕士项目副教授，目前住在新泽西州的维罗纳（Verona, New Jersey）。

肖内西的诗歌作品曾出现在《炸弹！美国最佳诗歌》（*Best American Poetry, BOMB*）、《连词》（*Conjunctions*）、《麦斯威尼》（*McSweeney's*）、《纽约客》、《巴黎评论》、《耶鲁评论》等杂志上。《我们的仙女座》（*Our Andromeda*, 2012）被《图书馆杂志》评为"年度图书"并被《纽约时报》评为"2013年100本最佳图书"之一，入围2013年笔会/开卷奖（PEN/Open Book Award）和2013年国际格里芬诗歌奖（International Griffin Poetry Prize）。此外她还出版了《章鱼博物馆》（*The Octopus Museum*, 2019）等多本诗集。

下文诗歌《假日》选自肖内西的诗集《我们的仙女座》，叙述了作者在假日中任由思想驰骋，享受悠闲时光。

作品选读

Our Andromeda

Vacation
for Mark and Paul

1
When the mind walks without language,
there is no boardwalk; there is no Board;
there is no boredom; and there are no feet,
legs or yards, coin or meter. No measure,
no miles. What is freedom if not freedom
from distance? From speaking lines?
2
The leaves, little green lamps for the sunblind.
3
Blue fingertips. Could mean a beach-party
manicure or a corpse. Or: and a corpse.
To be touched intimately by blue fingertips.
To put it more bluntly: to be fingered
by the pool in which you drown.
4
Why not sparkle if given a choice and you've
had enough sleep? Why not give back
a tiny grain of what you've been given from
night's endlessness and guaranteed breathing?
I have fractured only so minute a corner
of the deadest, most useless bone in the sky's
body, how can I not make a kite of it?
How can I keep even the broken glass
to myself, drinking nothing out of nothing?

5
To swim is to let ... know you won't take it
lying down nor will you just lie down and take it.
6
Solemn toes respond directly even to the most
frivolous mind. What other rules but bent
rules? Can I love you from the other
side of the conversation? From the other side
of the brown-feathered space of the table?
Of the living, eaten egg and sunrise and sleep-
eyes wet from night?
7
The tiny grain of sand in the eye. The single
flap that lands the bird into the lonely next,
the only nest in the sea. The glimmer that
proves contact has been made. Dear child,
wild sea, closed eye. Far, loving air.
8
Walking in the sand—am I under the sun
or dangling over it, first by one foot
and then the other?
9
This cerulean weather and its yellow talons.
The afternoon on the brink of drink. My ears
are plugged with wax and seawater, utterly
corked. The light has to widen to include
the music I can't hear. I am hoping the ...
of catastrophe—barbecue, lightning, riptide—
has smarter fish to fry. Suddenly the scruffy
deer appears, as it often does in poems, a dark-
eyed child dreaming in a dream.
10
Where oh where is that one leaf?

31
(Hanya Yanagihara, 1975—)
柳原垣谷

作者简介

柳原垣谷（Hanya Yanagihara, 1975—）是美国日裔著名小说家，出生于洛杉矶，她的父亲罗纳德·柳原（Ronald Yanagihara）来自夏威夷，母亲出生在首尔。柳原小时候与家人辗转于夏威夷、纽约、马里兰、加利福尼亚和得克萨斯等地。1995 年从史密斯学院毕业后，柳原搬到了纽约，并在那里做了几年撰稿人和编辑。她的第一部小说《树上的人》(*The People in the Trees*, 2013) 部分取材于病毒学家丹尼尔·卡尔顿·加杜塞克（Daniel Carleton Gajdusek）的真实案例，被誉为 2013 年最佳小说之一。她的小说《小生命》(*A Little Life*) 出版于 2015 年 3 月，获得了广泛好评。这本书入围了 2015 年布克小说奖，并获得了 2015 年科库斯小说奖（Kirkus Prize for fiction）。此外，柳原还被选为 2015 年国家图书奖小说单元的决选选手。她的第三部小说《到天堂去》(*To Paradise*) 于 2022 年 1 月出版。

在《小生命》中，柳原赞颂了一种悲剧性和超然的兄弟之爱，同时她还审视了记忆暴政和人类忍耐力的极限。来自马萨诸塞州一所小学院的四名同学搬到纽约开始他们的新生活：他们身无分文，生活漂泊不定，能够支撑他们的只有他们之间的友谊和对未来的远大抱负。四人当中，善良英俊的威廉是个有抱负的演员；杰比出生于布鲁克林，是个头脑敏捷、有时有些残忍的画家，想进入艺术界；马尔科姆是一家著名建筑公司的失意建筑师；而沉默寡言、才华横溢、神秘莫测的裘德则是四人的中心。多年来，他们的关系因毒品、成功和骄傲而密切或者疏远。

下文节选部分出自本书的第一章，叙述四个年轻人来到纽约开始新生活，一起商讨解决住宿问题。

作品选读

A Little Life

1
(Excertp)

  THE ELEVENTH APARTMENT had only one closet, but it did have a sliding glass door that opened onto a small balcony, from which he could see a man sitting across the way, outdoors in only a T-shirt and shorts even though it was October, smoking. Willem held up a hand in greeting to him, but the man didn't wave back.

  In the bedroom, Jude was accordioning the closet door, opening and shutting it, when Willem came in. "There's only one closet," he said.

  "That's okay," Willem said. "I have nothing to put in it anyway."

  "Neither do I." They smiled at each other. The agent from the building wandered in after them. "We'll take it," Jude told her.

  But back at the agent's office, they were told they couldn't rent the apartment after all. "Why not?" Jude asked her.

  "You don't make enough to cover six months' rent, and you don't have anything in savings," said the agent, suddenly terse. She had checked their credit and their bank accounts and had at last realized that there was something amiss about two men in their twenties who were not a couple and yet were trying to rent a one-bedroom apartment on a dull (but still expensive) stretch of Twenty-fifth Street. "Do you have anyone who can sign on as your guarantor? A boss? Parents?"

  "Our parents are dead," said Willem, swiftly.

  The agent sighed. "Then I suggest you lower your expectations. No one who manages a well-run building is going to rent to candidates with your financial profile." And then she stood, with an air of finality, and looked pointedly at the door.

  When they told JB and Malcolm this, however, they made it into a comedy: the apartment floor became tattooed with mouse droppings, the man across the way had almost exposed himself, the agent was upset because she had been flirting with Willem and he hadn't reciprocated.

"Who wants to live on Twenty-fifth and Second anyway," asked JB. They were at Pho Viet Huong in Chinatown, where they met twice a month for dinner. Pho Viet Huong wasn't very good—the pho was curiously sugary, the lime juice was soapy, and at least one of them got sick after every meal—but they kept coming, both out of habit and necessity. You could get a bowl of soup or a sandwich at Pho Viet Huong for five dollars, or you could get an entrée, which were eight to ten dollars but much larger, so you could save half of it for the next day or for a snack later that night. Only Malcolm never ate the whole of his entrée and never saved the other half either, and when he was finished eating, he put his plate in the center of the table so Willem and JB—who were always hungry—could eat the rest.

"Of course we don't want to live at Twenty-fifth and Second, JB," said Willem, patiently, "but we don't really have a choice. We don't have any money, remember?"

"I don't understand why you don't stay where you are," said Malcolm, who was now pushing his mushrooms and tofu—he always ordered the same dish: oyster mushrooms and braised tofu in a treacly brown sauce—around his plate, as Willem and JB eyed it.

"Well, I can't," Willem said. "Remember?" He had to have explained this to Malcolm a dozen times in the last three months. "Merritt's boyfriend's moving in, so I have to move out."

"But why do you have to move out?"

"Because it's Merritt's name on the lease, Malcolm!" said JB.

"Oh," Malcolm said. He was quiet. He often forgot what he considered inconsequential details, but he also never seemed to mind when people grew impatient with him for forgetting. "Right." He moved the mushrooms to the center of the table. "But you, Jude—"

"I can't stay at your place forever, Malcolm. Your parents are going to kill me at some point."

"My parents love you."

"That's nice of you to say. But they won't if I don't move out, and soon."

Malcolm was the only one of the four of them who lived at home, and as JB liked to say, if he had Malcolm's home, he would live at home too. It wasn't as if Malcolm's house was particularly grand—it was, in fact, creaky and ill-kept, and Willem had once gotten a splinter simply by running his hand up its banister—but it was large: a real Upper East Side town house. Malcolm's sister, Flora, who was three years older than him, had moved out of the basement apartment recently, and Jude had taken her place as a short-term solution: Eventually, Malcolm's parents would want to reclaim the unit to convert it into offices for his mother's literary agency, which meant Jude (who was finding the flight of stairs that led down to it too difficult to navigate anyway) had to look for his own apartment.

And it was natural that he would live with Willem; they had been roommates throughout college. In their first year, the four of them had shared a space that consisted of a cinder-blocked common room, where sat their desks and chairs and a couch that JB's aunts had driven up in a U-Haul, and a second, far tinier room, in which two sets of bunk beds had been placed. This room had been so narrow that Malcolm and Jude, lying in the bottom bunks, could reach out and grab each other's hands. Malcolm and JB had shared one of the units; Jude and Willem had shared the other.

"It's blacks versus whites," JB would say.

"Jude's not white," Willem would respond.

"And I'm not black," Malcolm would add, more to annoy JB than because he believed it.

"Well," JB said now, pulling the plate of mushrooms toward him with the tines of his fork, "I'd say you could both stay with me, but I think you'd fucking hate it." JB lived in a massive, filthy loft in Little Italy, full of strange hallways that led to unused, oddly shaped cul-de-sacs and unfinished half rooms, the Sheetrock abandoned mid-construction, which belonged to another person they knew from college. Ezra was an artist, a bad one, but he didn't need to be good because, as JB liked to remind them, he would never have to work: They could make bad, unsalable, worthless art for generations and they would still be able to buy at whim the best oils they wanted, and impractically large lofts in downtown Manhattan that they could trash with their bad architectural decisions, and when they got sick of the artist's life—as JB was convinced Ezra someday would—all they would need to do is call their trust officers and be awarded an enormous lump sum of cash of an amount that the four of them (well, maybe not Malcolm) could never dream of seeing in their lifetimes. In the meantime, though, Ezra was a useful person to know, not only because he let JB and a few of his other friends from school stay in his apartment—at any time, there were four or five people burrowing in various corners of the loft—but because he was a good-natured and basically generous person, and liked to throw excessive parties in which copious amounts of food and drugs and alcohol were available for free.

"Hold up," JB said, putting his chopsticks down. "I just realized—there's someone at the magazine renting some place for her aunt. Like, just on the verge of Chinatown."

"How much is it?" asked Willem.

"Probably nothing—she didn't even know what to ask for it. And she wants someone in there that she knows."

"Do you think you could put in a good word?"

"Better—I'll introduce you. Can you come by the office tomorrow?"

Jude sighed. "I won't be able to get away." He looked at Willem.

"Don't worry—I can. What time?"

"Lunchtime, I guess. One?"

"I'll be there."

Willem was still hungry, but he let JB eat the rest of the mushrooms. Then they all waited around for a bit; sometimes Malcolm ordered jackfruit ice cream, the one consistently good thing on the menu, ate two bites, and then stopped, and he and JB would finish the rest. But this time he didn't order the ice cream, and so they asked for the bill so they could study it and divide it to the dollar.

32

(Yuko Taniguchi, 1975—)
谷口裕子

作者简介

谷口裕子（Yuko Taniguchi, 1975—）出生于日本横滨，是著名美国日裔诗人、小说家。她毕业于圣本笃学院（College of Saint Benedict）和圣约翰大学（Saint John's University），并在明尼苏达大学获得艺术硕士学位（University of Minnesota）。目前她在明尼苏达大学教书。在日常授课和写作的间隙，她也与作家、艺术家和医疗保健专业人员一起探讨治疗和创造性过程的交集。她目前正在开展一些实践活动，以促进那些与心理健康问题作斗争的青少年的参与感和灵感。谷口目前出版了一部诗集《外籍妻子的挽歌》（*Foreign Wife Elegy*, 2004）和一部小说《壁橱里的海洋》（*The Ocean in the Closet*, 2007）。2008年她获得了由前哥伦布基金会颁发的美国图书奖，以及桐山环太平洋图书奖杰出著作（Kiriyama Prize Notable Book）；进入过代顿文学和平奖（Dayton Literary Peace Prize）和第11届美国亚裔文学奖的决选名单。

下文节选诗歌是她2004年《外籍妻子的挽歌》诗集中的同名诗歌，叙述了一位外籍妻子希望丈夫学习自己的语言以便将自己因车祸去世的消息告知母亲。

作品选读

Foreign Wife Elegy

My language has its own world
where he doesn't know how to live,
but he should learn my language;
then he can call my mother to say
that I am dead. I drive too fast
and someone else drives too fast
and we crash on the icy road.
The death sweeps me away.
He can tell this to my mother
if he learns my language.
Her large yellow voice travels
and hits his body, but at least she knows
that I am dead, and if I die,
I want him to tell my mother
with his deep voice shaking.

33
(Katie Kitamura, 1979—)
凯蒂·北村

作者简介

凯蒂·北村（Katie Kitamura，1979— ）出生于加州萨克拉门托的一个日裔家庭，在戴维斯长大。北村于1999年毕业于新泽西州普林斯顿大学。2005年她获得了美国文学博士学位，论文题目为《粗俗美学与美国现代小说》（"The Aesthetics of Vulgarity and the Modern American Novel"）。北村为《卫报》、《纽约时报》和《连线》撰稿，写过武术、电影评论和分析以及艺术方面的文章。北村的作品包括《游客眼中的日本——一段旅程》（*Japanese for Travellers—A Journey*, 2006），以及小说《长枪》（*The Longshot: A Novel*, 2009）、《到森林去》（*Gone to the Forest*, 2013）、《别离》（*A Separation*, 2017）和《亲密无间》（*Intimacies*, 2021）。北村的小说颇受欢迎。《长枪》在2010年入围了纽约公共图书馆的青年雄狮小说奖（New York Public Library's Young Lions Fiction Award）。2013年，她的小说《到森林去》同样入围了该奖项。2021年，她的小说《亲密关系》入围了美国国家图书奖小说奖。

《亲密关系》叙述了一个女性辗转于诸多真相之间的扣人心弦的故事。一名口译员逃离纽约来到海牙，在国际法院工作。作为一个拥有多种语言和身份的女人，她正在寻找一个可以称之为家园的地方。她陷入了不断升温的个人闹剧：她的情人阿德里安（Adriaan）与妻子分居，但仍被婚姻纠缠；她的朋友吉娜（Jana）目睹了一场看似随意的暴力行为；她还因为为一位被控犯有战争罪的前总统做翻译被卷入了政治事件中。但是对真理和爱的追求使她从自己的生活中得到了解脱。

下文节选自小说的第二章，描述叙事者在海牙的生活和工作状况，重点是作为一位同声传译员应该如何工作。

作品选读

Intimacies

2
(Excerpt)

I lived in the city center, in a very different neighborhood to Jana's. Prior to my arrival, I had found my furnished apartment by way of online listings. The Hague was not a cheap city to live in, but it was cheaper than New York. As a result, I lived in an apartment that was too big for one person, with two bedrooms and separate dining and living rooms.

It took me some time to grow accustomed to the size of the apartment, an effect exacerbated by the furnishings, which were somehow too perfunctory for its proportions. A foldout futon in the living room, a compact dinette in the dining room, the space was designed to be both temporary and impersonal. When I signed the lease I had considered that vacancy a luxury, I remember walking through the apartment, my footsteps hollow, marking one room the bedroom, another a possible study. In time that feeling faded, and the dimensions of the apartment no longer seemed remarkable. Nor did the interim nature of the accommodation, although when I returned that evening from Jana's, I recalled the ease with which she'd seemed to inhabit her apartment, and felt a ripple of vague longing.

When I woke the next morning it was still dark outside. I made a coffee and pulled on a coat and went out onto the balcony—another feature of the apartment, one that I used even during these frigid winter months. I had wedged a small table and a single folding chair against the wall, along with a few potted plants, now withered. I sat down. It was early enough that the streets below were empty. The Hague was a quiet city, and almost strenuously civilized. But the more time I spent there, the more its air of courtesy, the preserved buildings and manicured parks, imparted a sense of unease. I recalled what Jana had said about living in The Hague, how it inured you to what a real city was like. This was possibly true, increasingly I'd begun to think the docile surface of the city concealed a more complex and contradictory nature.

Only last week, I had been shopping in the Old Town when I saw three uniformed men moving down the busy pedestrian street alongside a large machine. Two of the men held slender picks while the third held a large nozzle that protruded from the machine, the effect was rather as if he were leading an elephant by the trunk. I had paused to observe them without really knowing why, perhaps only because I wondered what manner of slow-moving work they were doing.

They eventually approached and I could see exactly the task they were performing, the two men with the picks were carefully extracting cigarette butts from between the cracks of the cobbled road, one by one by one, painstaking labor that explained their sluggish pace of progress. I looked down and realized that the road was strewn with cigarette butts, this despite the fact that there were several well-placed public ashtrays on that stretch of street alone. The two men continued to flip the cigarette butts out of the cracks while the third man followed with his elephantine vacuum, dutifully sucking up the debris with the machine, the drum of which presumably held many thousands or even hundreds of thousands of cigarette butts, each of which had been disappeared from the street by the work of these men.

The three men were almost certainly immigrants, possibly Turkish and Surinamese. Meanwhile, their labor was necessitated by the heritage aesthetic of the city, not to mention the carelessness of a wealthy population that dropped its cigarette butts onto the pavement without a thought, when the designated receptacle was only a few feet away, I now saw that there were dozens of cigarette butts on the ground directly below the ashtrays. It was only an anecdote. But it was one example of how the city's veneer of civility was constantly giving way, in places it was barely there at all.

Around me the light was beginning to come up, color blotting the horizon. I went inside and dressed for work. I left the apartment not long after, I was now running late. I hurried to the nearby tram stop. Jana called me while I was waiting. She was still at home and I could hear her moving through the apartment, collecting her keys and gathering her books and papers. She asked if I had made it home safely and I assured her that the journey had passed without incident. There was a pause, I heard the slam of a door. She was on her way out of her building and into the street. She sounded distracted, almost as if she could not remember why she had called, then she reminded me that I was bringing Adriaan to her house for dinner on Saturday, and asked if there was anything in particular he did or did not eat.

The tram was arriving and I told her that anything would be fine, and that I would call her later. I hung up and boarded the tram and was soon jolting toward the Court, where I was now nearly six months into my contract. Most of my colleagues had lived in multiple countries and were cosmopolitan in nature, their identity indivisible from their linguistic capabilities. I qualified in much the same way. I had native fluency in English and Japanese from my parents, and in French from a childhood in Paris. I had also studied Spanish and German to the point of professional proficiency, although these along with Japanese were less essential than English and French, the working languages of the Court.

But fluency was merely the foundation for any kind of interpretive work, which demanded extreme precision, and I often thought that it was my natural inclination toward the latter, rather than any linguistic aptitude, that made me a good interpreter. That exactitude was even more important in a legal context, and within a week of working at the Court I learned that its vocabulary was both specific and arcane, with official terminology that was set in each language, and then closely followed by all the interpreters on the team. This was done for obvious reasons, there were great chasms beneath words, between two or sometimes more languages, that could open up without warning.

As interpreters it was our job to throw down planks across these gaps. That navigation—which alongside accuracy required a certain amount of native spontaneity, at times you had to improvise in order to rapidly parse a difficult phrase, you were always working against the clock—was more significant than you might initially think. With inconsistent interpretation, for example, a reliable witness could appear unreliable, seeming to change his or her testimony with each new interpreter. This in turn could affect the outcome of a trial, the judges were unlikely to note a change of personnel in the interpreters' booth, even if the voice speaking in their ears suddenly became markedly different, switching from male to female, from halting to deliberate.

They would only note the change in their perception of the witness. A sliver of unreliability introducing fractures into the testimony of the witness, those fractures would develop into cracks, which would in turn threaten the witness's entire persona. Every person who took to the stand was projecting an image of one kind or another: their testimony was heavily coached and shaped by either the defense or the prosecution, they had been brought to the Court in order to perform a role. The Court was run according to the suspension of disbelief: every person in the courtroom knew but also did not know that there was a great deal of artifice surrounding matters that were nonetheless predicated on authenticity.

In the Court, what was at stake was nothing less than the suffering of thousands of people, and in suffering there could be no question of pretense. And yet the Court was by nature a place of high theatrics. It was not only in the carefully crafted testimony of the victims. The first time I attended a session I had been startled, both the prosecution and the defense had been unmeasured in pleading their cases. And then the accused themselves were often grandiose in character, both imperious and self-pitying, they were politicians and generals, people used to occupying a large stage and hearing the sound of their own voices. The interpreters couldn't entirely eschew these dramatics, it was our job not only to interpret the words the subject was speaking, but also to express or indicate the demeanor, the nuance and intention behind their words.

The first time you listened to an interpreter speaking, their voice might sound cold and precise and completely without inflection, but the longer you listened, the more variation you would hear. If a joke was made it was the interpreter's job to communicate the humor or attempt at humor; similarly, when something was said ironically it was important to indicate that the words were not to be taken at face value. Linguistic accuracy was not enough. Interpretation was a matter of great subtlety, a word with many contexts, for example it is often said that an actor interprets a role, or a musician a piece of music.

There was a certain level of tension that was intrinsic to the Court and its activities, a contradiction between the intimate nature of pain, and the public arena in which it had to be exhibited. A trial was a complex calculus of performance in which we were all involved, and from which none of us could be entirely exempt. It was the job of the interpreter not simply to state or perform but to repeat the unspeakable. Perhaps that was the real anxiety within the Court, and among the interpreters. The fact that our daily activity hinged on the repeated description—description, elaboration, and delineation—of matters that were, outside, generally subject to euphemism and elision.

34

(Phil Kaye, 1987—)
菲尔·凯伊

作者简介

菲尔·凯伊（Phil Kaye, 1987—）出生在加州，母亲是日本人，父亲是犹太裔美国人。他是美国日裔诗人、作家和电影制作人。凯伊的家庭以及他的日本和犹太血统是他作品中反复出现的主题。凯伊17岁时开始表演口语诗歌，随后他继续在布朗大学就读，在那里他加入了一个诗歌俱乐部，并最终在2011年参加了全国诗歌大满贯决赛。目前他出版了两本书：《电灯泡交响曲》（*A Light Bulb Symphony*, 2011）和《日期与时间》（*Date & Time*, 2018）。凯伊目前住在纽约市。

诗集《电灯泡交响曲》主题包括凯伊的家庭生活、祖先和祖父的故事。而《日期与时间》则探索与记忆、家庭和孤独相关的主题，讲述了一个个温馨的故事，让读者感同身受，生活在最美好的时刻。

选文《大黄峰》（"Camaro"）是其诗集《日期与时间》中的一首，作者回忆自己与友人开着租赁的大黄峰汽车旅行的往事。

作品选读

Date & Time

Camaro

you & I are standing
at the Hertz Rent-a-Car counter
& you are trying to convince me
to rent a convertible

you say
an extra hundred bucks
won't be something
we remember years
from now

you
are wrong
I remember

but also right
in the way you often are
◊
that afternoon
we drive down the coast of California
in a white convertible Camaro

three hours south of San Francisco is Big Sur
a place where the cliffs cleave into the Pacific Ocean
& we drive on the edge of the blade

I look over at you

hair whipping back in a wind
you bargained for

I want to say something
but I do not know what
◊
In elementary school I had a crush
from 1st to 3rd grade
and she left school one day in the middle of the year
on a normal Tuesday
& did not come back
I never said a word to her
◊
in the convertible
you tell me
you like how thoughtfully I choose my words
how I am comfortable in silence
I say
I love you
◊
that afternoon we come upon wet cement on the sidewalk
first we giggle
ready to write our names
fingers out
two aliens
phoning home

then we stop
talk about
how it would be insensitive
how this is not our block
keep walking
do not hold hands
do not talk about writing

our names next to each other
what it means to let that harden
◊
months later
we are at a restaurant
in New York City
where it is never silent
but our corner is quiet
for a long time

you say
adventure is important to me now
& you leave
on a normal Tuesday
& do not come back
◊
I return to the places we went
looking for something
like a tourist trespassing in a Hollywood neighborhood
hoping to spot a star on their front lawn
for just a few seconds
I speak to many people
in many places
speak through a microphone
so that I cannot hear anything else
◊
months later
we see each other

you tell me
you look like you're doing okay
you tell me
you did so many things right
you tell me

I don't know what to say

I nod in agreement
& for a moment we are again
together
two aliens trying to find home

& then you leave
& I ask questions to an empty room

do you remember the cliffs?
the woman with the side ponytail at the rental car counter?
the hundred bucks?
how you thought we wouldn't remember
any of this
years from now

I remember

35

(Sarah Kay, 1988—)
莎拉·凯

作者简介

莎拉·凯（Sarah Kay, 1988—）出生在纽约市，母亲是美国日裔，父亲是犹太人。她拥有布朗大学的文学硕士学位，以及格林内尔学院（Grinnell College）的人文文学荣誉博士学位。她现在写诗，读诗，并为不同的观众表演诗歌，也是她目前从事的项目 VOICE 的联合导演和创始人。14 岁时，她开始表演诗歌，参加过许多诗歌比赛，是在得克萨斯州奥斯汀举行的国家诗歌大满贯比赛中最年轻的选手。2007 年，凯首次在电视上亮相，也曾在林肯中心（Lincoln Center）、翠贝卡电影节（Tribeca Film Festival）以及联合国 2004 年世界青年报告（World Youth Report）发布会上担任特约演员。虽然凯的作品主要是口语诗，但她也出版了几部诗集：《B》（B, 2011）、《不管残骸如何》（No Matter the Wreckage, 2014）、《类型》（The Type, 2016）以及《我们所有激动人心的奇迹》（All Our Wild Wonder, 2018）。

《不管残骸如何》是凯收集她诗歌创作生涯第一个十年诗歌作品的选集，为读者呈现了许多受欢迎的新作品，展示了她在庆祝家庭、爱情、旅行、历史和无生命物体以及其他有趣的话题方面的技巧。凯的诗清新而睿智，将读者带入她的旅程，与其一起探索发现她周围的世界。下文《手》一诗为诗集中的一首，作者认为手握紧后成为拳头可以对他人施加暴力而与政治联系起来。

作品选读

No Matter the Wreckage

Hands

People used to tell me that I had beautiful hands.
They told me so often, in fact, that one day I started to
believe them; I started listening. Until I asked my
photographer father, Hey Daddy, could I be a hand model?
To which Dad laughed and said, No way.
I don't remember the reason he gave,
and it probably didn't matter anyway.
I would have been upset, but there were
far too many crayons to grab, too many
stuffed animals to hold, too many ponytails to tie,
too many homework assignments to write,
too many boys to wave at, too many years to grow.
We used to have a game, my dad and I, about holding hands.
We held hands everywhere. In the car, on the bus, on the street,
at a movie. And every time, either he or I would whisper a
great big number to the other, pretending that we were
keeping track of how many times we had held hands,
that we were sure this one had to be eight-million,
two-thousand, seven-hundred and fifty-three.
Hands learn. More than minds do.
Hands learn how to hold other hands.
How to grip pencils and mold poetry.
How to memorize computer keys
and telephone buttons in the dark.
How to tickle pianos and grip bicycle handles.
How to dribble a basketball and how to peel apart

pages of Sunday comics that somehow always seem to stick together.
They learn how to touch old people and how to hold babies.
I love hands like I love people. They are the maps and
compasses with which we navigate our way through life,
feeling our way over mountains passed and valleys crossed;
they are our histories.
Some people read palms to tell your future,
I read hands to tell your past.
Each scar marks a story worth telling. Each callused palm,
each cracked knuckle, is a broken bottle, a missed punch,
a rusty nail, years in a factory.
Now, I watch Middle Eastern hands
clenched in Middle Eastern fists.
Pounding against each other like war drums,
each country sees their fists as warriors,
and others as enemies, even if fists alone are only hands.
But this is not a poem about politics; hands are not about politics.
This is a poem about love.
And fingers. Fingers interlocked like a beautiful accordion of flesh
or a zipper of prayer. One time, I grabbed my dad's hand
so that our fingers interlocked perfectly, but he changed his
position, saying, No, that hand-hold is for your mom.
Kids high five, sounds of hand-to-hand combat
instead mark camaraderie and teamwork.
Now, grown up, we learn to shake hands.
You need a firm handshake, but not too tight, don't be limp now,
don't drop too soon, but for …'s sake don't hold on too long…
but…hands are not about politics?
When did it become so complicated?
I always thought it simple.
The other day, my dad looked at my hands, as if seeing them
for the first time. And with laughter behind his eyelids,
with all the seriousness a man of his humor could muster, he said,
You've got nice hands. You could've been a hand model.

And before the laughter can escape me,
I shake my head at him,
and squeeze his hand.
Eight-million, two-thousand, seven-hundred and fifty-four.

中国人民大学出版社外语出版分社读者信息反馈表

尊敬的读者：

　　感谢您购买和使用中国人民大学出版社外语出版分社的 ＿＿＿＿＿＿＿ 一书，我们希望通过这张小小的反馈卡来获得您更多的建议和意见，以改进我们的工作，加强我们双方的沟通和联系。我们期待着能为更多的读者提供更多的好书。

　　请您填妥下表后，寄回或传真回复我们，对您的支持我们不胜感激！

1. 您是从何种途径得知本书的：
   □书店　　　□网上　　　□报纸杂志　　　□朋友推荐
2. 您为什么决定购买本书：
   □工作需要　□学习参考　□对本书主题感兴趣　□随便翻翻
3. 您对本书内容的评价是：
   □很好　　　□好　　　□一般　　　□差　　　□很差
4. 您在阅读本书的过程中有没有发现明显的专业及编校错误，如果有，它们是：
   ＿＿＿＿＿＿＿＿＿＿＿＿＿＿＿＿＿＿＿＿＿＿＿＿＿＿＿＿＿＿＿＿＿＿
   ＿＿＿＿＿＿＿＿＿＿＿＿＿＿＿＿＿＿＿＿＿＿＿＿＿＿＿＿＿＿＿＿＿＿
   ＿＿＿＿＿＿＿＿＿＿＿＿＿＿＿＿＿＿＿＿＿＿＿＿＿＿＿＿＿＿＿＿＿＿

5. 您对哪些专业的图书信息比较感兴趣：
   ＿＿＿＿＿＿＿＿＿＿＿＿＿＿＿＿＿＿＿＿＿＿＿＿＿＿＿＿＿＿＿＿＿＿
   ＿＿＿＿＿＿＿＿＿＿＿＿＿＿＿＿＿＿＿＿＿＿＿＿＿＿＿＿＿＿＿＿＿＿
   ＿＿＿＿＿＿＿＿＿＿＿＿＿＿＿＿＿＿＿＿＿＿＿＿＿＿＿＿＿＿＿＿＿＿

6. 如果方便，请提供您的个人信息，以便于我们和您联系（您的个人资料我们将严格保密）：
   您供职的单位：＿＿＿＿＿＿＿＿＿＿＿＿＿＿＿＿＿＿＿＿＿＿＿＿＿＿
   您教授的课程（教师填写）：＿＿＿＿＿＿＿＿＿＿＿＿＿＿＿＿＿＿＿＿
   您的通信地址：＿＿＿＿＿＿＿＿＿＿＿＿＿＿＿＿＿＿＿＿＿＿＿＿＿＿
   您的电子邮箱：＿＿＿＿＿＿＿＿＿＿＿＿＿＿＿＿＿＿＿＿＿＿＿＿＿＿

请联系我们：黄婷　程子殊　吴振良　王琼　鞠方安

电话：010-62512737，62513265，62515538，62515573，62515576

传真：010-62514961

E-mail：huangt@crup.com.cn　　chengzsh@crup.com.cn　　wuzl@crup.com.cn
　　　　crup_wy@163.com　　jufa@crup.com.cn

通信地址：北京市海淀区中关村大街甲59号文化大厦15层　　邮编：100872

中国人民大学出版社外语出版分社